HAWK

A Western Novel

By

Dusty Rhodes

HAWK

Copyright © 2012
By Dusty Rhodes
All rights reserved

Cover design by Julie Sartain

Published by Dusty Rhodes Books in USA
The characters and events in this book are fictional.
Any resemblance to persons either living or dead is
strictly coincidental.

All rights are reserved. No part of this book may be
reproduced or transmitted in any form by any means
electronic or mechanical. This includes photocopying,
recording, scanning to a compact disc, or by
Any informational storage and retrieval system, without
the express written permission of Dusty Rhodes.

ISBN : 978-1-4675-1309-8

Other Books by Dusty Rhodes
MANHUNTER
SHILOH
JEDIDIAH BOONE
SHOOTER
DEATH RIDES A PALE HORSE
VENGEANCE IS MINE
LONGHORN BOOK I (sub title) THE BEGINNING
LONGHORN BOOK II (sub title) THE HONDO KID
LONGHORN BOOK III (sub title) THE PRODIGAL BROTHER
LONGHORN BOOK IV (sub title) THE FAMILY
SHAWGO
SHAWGO II
CHERO
THE TOWN TAMER
DEATH ANGEL
HAWK

To Order
Simply cut or tear out the EZ-ORDER FORM in back of book, make your selections, attach your check, and drop it in the mail. We will ship your books within three working days from receipt of order.

MAIL YOUR ORDER TO:
Dusty Rhodes
P. O. Box 7
Greenwood, AR 72936

Or Order On-Line
www.dustyrhodesbooks.com

Audio Books (on CD's) and E-Books for E-Book Readers are available On-Line.

HAWK

HAWK

A western novel
By
Dusty Rhodes

CHAPTER I

Jubal Hawk was bone tired.

He slouched his tall, six foot frame wearily in his McClellan saddle and heeled his weary buckskin, Buck, to pick up the pace as he drew near the entrance to the long, winding lane that led to his home—home—just the thought of being back home sent a surge of overwhelming emotion rushing through him.

It had been almost five years since he left to fight for a cause he was willing to die for—a cause now lost with the surrender of the Confederate forces by General Robert E. Lee at Appomattox, April 9th, 1865.

He fought proudly as a captain in the First Virginia Cavalry; Forty-Third Battalion, under the command of John Mosby. Known for their lightning-fast raids and their ability to vanish, seemingly into thin air, they became known as *Mosby's Raiders* and their commander was called the *Gray Ghost* by the Union commanders.

As he had done many times in the previous weeks during his long ride, he forced the painful memories of the war from his mind and turned his thoughts to his folks and the homecoming that awaited him. His last memory of his mother was when he turned in his saddle to wave *good-bye*. She was standing on the wide front porch of the large, white, two-story home where he had spent the first nineteen years of his life. Arm in arm with his father, both had been crying at his departure—it was the first time he had seen his father shed tears.

Mary Lou, his twelve year old sister stood beside them; she too, was crying. Jason, his brother, five years younger than Jubal, had begged to go with him, but had been denied permission by their father.

The memory of that picture had been uppermost in his mind during the long four years of the war and had helped to sustain him during many fierce battles and untold lonely nights.

But that was all over now—now he could get back to doing what he loved to do—raising and training Tennessee Walking horses on their sprawling, five hundred acre ranch.

He rounded the wooded bend and looked up the lane. His heart stopped beating!

A huge knot raced up into his throat and lodged there. His eyes bugged wide and his mouth dropped agape.

It wasn't there!—his home wasn't there!

Nothing but a charred pile of timbers and rocks from the chimney remained.

He dug heels into Buck's flanks and sent him into a hard gallop. Jubal's mind raced, his mind flooded with a thousand questions.

His chest hurt—he had trouble breathing.

Where were his folks—his family?

As he drew nearer he saw the horse barns, or what was left of them, lying in a pile of ashes and twisted and rusty sheet iron. The rails of their corrals lay scattered on the ground near the former barns.

Jubal's slow gaze scanned the tragic scene in stunned disbelief. He was shocked by the loss of his former home, but his primary concern was for his family.

Where are they?
What has happened to them?
Who could have done this?

He slowly dismounted and dropped the reins of his buckskin, ground hitching him. He swept the area with a slow, searching gaze.

He walked slowly to the remains of the house, pausing to pick up a half-charred board. He poked around in the ashes, hoping against hope to find something—anything that might give him a clue as to what happened.

"Master Jubal, sir!" a familiar voice called from a distance. "Is dat you?"

Jubal swung an excited look at the voice. A tall, husky, elderly black man emerged from a thick stand of pine trees half-a-hundred yards away.

"Wash?" Jubal shouted, emotion cracking his voice. "Wash? Is that you?"

His booted feet carried him swiftly to meet the faithful servant who had served the Hawk family for as long as Jubal could remember.

"I'm so glad to see you! You're a sight for sore eyes!" Jubal greeted, wrapping his big arms around the black man.

"Shore mighty good to see you too, sir!"

Jubal stood back and looked at the big Negro through tear-blurred eyes. His faded and tattered overalls hung by one shoulder strap. He wore no shirt or shoes, but wore a wide, white-toothed smile.

"I see'd you coming, Master Jubal. I thinks it was you, but you shore have grown some. I couldn't be shore with all the meanness goings on around here."

"Meanness? What kind of *meanness?* Where are my folks, Wash? What happened here?"

"It was bad, Master Jubal, sir, mighty bad! The bad men, they comes in the middle of the night with their toe-sack hoods hidin' their faces. They burned the barns first. Master Hawk tried to stop them, but they beat him with clubs and hung him right there from that big ole oak tree. Me and Master Jason fought them, but they beat us with clubs and left us on the ground under your pappy's feet. Then they burned the house. We buried Master Hawk over yonder with the rest of your kin. That was all we knowed to do."

"You did the right thing," Jubal assured him, fighting back the tears that buffeted his eyelids and the sick feeling in his stomach.

"What about my mother and my family?" he asked anxiously. "What happened to them?"

"Missus Hawk said us slaves was free now and we could do whatever we wanted. The others left, but I decided to stay here. One of the wagons didn't burn so she took it and said she and the youngin's was goin' to her sister's."

"Yes, that would be Aunt Audrey down near Pigeon Forge."

He tried unsuccessfully to swallow the huge lump lodged in his throat. "Who was it, Wash? Who did this?"

"I don't know, Master Jubal, sir. Like I say, they all wore toe-sack hoods with holes cut to see through. They was mean, Master Jubal, bad mean. One of them rode a big black and white pinto is all I knows."

"A black and white pinto, huh?"

"Yes, sir. That's all I know."

"When did all this happen? How long ago?"

"It's been a long while, sir, I plumb lost track of time— a few months I reckon."

"If she set you free, why are you still here?"

"I didn't ask to be set free, sir. Working fer your family is all I knowed since I was a little tad, no bigger than nothin'. Missus Hawk tried to get me to go with her, but I didn't think that would be right. I'd just be another mouth to feed. That's all I knows, sir."

"Where you staying now?"

"I sleeps in the bushes yonder and in the storm cellar when it gets cold and rainy."

"I'm gonna ride into town and see what's going on. I'll bring back some supplies."

"I be waitin' Master Jubal, sir. I be right here waitin'."

Jubal walked slowly over to the small plot of ground that was surrounded by a wrought-iron fence; they had set it aside to bury the family. A fresh mound of dirt identified his father's grave. A small wooden cross stood at the head of the grave. Jubal knelt to one knee and placed an open hand on the fresh earth.

Emotions welled up inside him. Large tears breached his eyelids and trailed across his whiskered face. He slowly shook his head.

"I'm sorry, Pa. I'm sorry I wasn't here to help you." He choked out the hoarse, whispered words.

Jubal set out for the nearest town, Sweetwater, Tennessee, some twelve miles west of the Hawk ranch. He intended to have a talk with the county sheriff about his father being hanged and their home being burned.

Sweetwater was a small town, having been established in the early 1850s by Isaac Lenoir, son of the late William Lenoir, a close friend of Jubal's father. The sheriff was a man by the name of Ben Lambert, also a longtime friend of the Hawk family.

As he rode into town he was surprised how much the town had grown in the five years he had been gone. He couldn't help noticing the long stares he drew as he rode down the street.

Most likely the remnants of the tattered and dirty Confederate captain's uniform he was still wearing, his whiskered face, and his long neglected, corn-silk hair and Confederate Cavalry hat.

He reined up in front of the sheriff's office and stepped down. He strode to the door and opened it. An unfamiliar fellow wearing a badge pinned to his vest sat behind the desk.

"I'm looking for Sheriff Lambert," he told the stranger behind the desk.

The man gave him a slow, hard look of disdain from head to toe and snarled out an answer.

"Lambert ain't the sheriff any more. I'm Sheriff Sam Bullock. Something I can do for you, *Reb*?"

"I'm Jubal Hawk. I just returned from the war to learn my father was hung a few months back and our house and barns on the Hawk Ranch were burned to the ground. I want to know who done it and if they've been punished for what they done?"

"Yeah, your ma come in awhile back rantin' and ravin' with some cock and bull story about *night-riders* with toe-sack hoods over their faces burning her house and hanging her husband. I rode out there a few days later and looked into it. I didn't see no evidence of *night-riders* or of anybody getting hung."

"That's because he was already buried. You saw the house and barns burned, didn't you?"

"Yeah, but as far as I know, anybody could have done that—even your own ma."

"My mother never told a lie in her whole life!" Jubal said angrily.

"How would I know? All I can go by is evidence and I didn't see anything to support her story. I don't put much stock in some woman runnin' around making up yarns to cover up a fire she most likely set herself. I go by evidence and there weren't none—end of story."

Anger welled up inside Jubal. He felt his face flush and his jaw set. His teeth clamped together and his fists clenched until his fingernails cut into the palms of his hands. He fought back the urge to lunge forward and vent his anger upon the lawman.

"No, *Sheriff*. That ain't the end of the story by a long shot. If you won't do your job I'll do it for you! I aim to find out who hung my father and burned our house and barns and stole our herd of horses!"

"Whoa, there, *Reb*! You just hold on right there!" the red-faced *sheriff* shouted, leaping to his feet. "*I'm* the law in this county. You go botherin' decent folks in my county and I'll stick you so far in jail you won't see daylight until you're a old man! Am I making myself clear?"

Jubal clenched his teeth and fought back the urge to bust the *so-called sheriff* in the mouth. Instead, he turned on his heels, and stormed from the office, slamming the door behind him.

He walked directly across the street to the Sweetwater Bank. He was still fuming when he walked into Mr. Stringfellow's office. The banker had been a business partner with his father and a friend of the Hawk family for years.

"Jubal Hawk!" the president of the bank said cheerfully, rising and hurrying around the desk with a wide smile and outstretched hand. "It's good to see you. You've grown up since I saw you last. Last time I saw you, you was still wet behind the ears. Now here you are a strapping six foot that could fight a mountain grizzly with your bare hands. When did you get back?"

"Just today," Jubal said, still upset from his encounter with the sheriff. "War has a way of either making a man or breaking a man. What do you know about my father being hung by *night-riders* and our house and barns being burned?"

"Yes, I heard about that. Your mother was in a few months ago and told me about it. I'm sorry, Jubal. Your father was a fine man and a better friend. There have been several instances of similar things happening around the county, mostly to Confederate sympathizers like your folks. Emotions over the war are still running high around here."

"And you've got yourself a sheriff that won't even bother to look into it."

"Yes, I'm sorry to say you're right. He's bought and paid for. But the town council of Sweetwater put him in office, with the strong recommendation of Colonel Jessup, of course. It was a big mistake, but we realized it too late.

"The Colonel's the big bull in Monroe County now. He's buying up everything he can get his hands on. Seems he's dead-set on owning the whole county. What he can't buy he seems to end up with one way or another. He's been after the bank ever since he came to Monroe County. Luckily, I still own controlling interest since I bought out your father's stock."

"My father sold his stock in the bank? When did this happen?"

"Your mother sold it to me at the same time she drew out all their money and closed their account. She said she was moving out of Monroe County and needed the money."

"So we've got no money in the bank now?"

"No, son, I'm afraid not, but if you need some money to tide you over until you get back on your feet, I can loan you whatever you need."

"No, that won't be necessary, but I'm obliged. Well, I won't bother you further then. Good day to you, Mr. Stringfellow."

"Good to see you again, Jubal. Will you be living out at the ranch?"

"Yes, not much there right now, but there will be again."

He left the bank and headed for the Sweetwater General Store up the street to get some supplies for him and Wash.

"Well, lookie here!" Mr. Hamburg said as Jubal walked in. "If it ain't Jubal Hawk. I almost didn't recognize you. You've been gone a long time, boy, four, five years maybe?"

"Yes, sir. It's been almost five years."

"Well, it's good to have you back. I heard about your pa. Sure sorry to hear it. Lots of bad things going on around here lately."

"Yeah, so I hear. I need to pick up a few supplies."

"Of course, just pick out what you need."

Jubal gathered up some basic supplies for him and Wash. He piled his purchases on the counter as the store owner added them up.

"That all comes to eighteen dollars and twenty cents."

Jubal reached in his pocket and pulled out his leather money pouch. He selected some bills and laid them on the counter. The store owner looked down at the money and then up at Jubal with a frown on his face.

"I'm sorry, Jubal, but we can't accept Confederate money any longer. It ain't worth the paper it's printed on."

The news hit Jubal like a horse kicking him in the stomach.

"But that's all I got," he told the store owner. "We need those supplies."

"I'm sorry."

Jubal nodded and walked from the store empty-handed.

What am I gonna do? He thought as he walked to his horse. *Mother's several days' ride away with all our money. I don't have nothing except Confederate money the army paid me and it's no good any more. I need supplies for me and Wash to get by on.*

His stomach was already cramping from lack of food during the two week ride from Virginia; now, here he was without a penny to his name.

As he mounted and headed out of town he suddenly thought of Mary Ann Morrison. They had sparked a little the last year or so before he left for the war. Most of their friends had always assumed they would marry when the war was over. He and her folks had always gotten along well, maybe...

The Morrisons lived on a small farm not far out of Sweetwater. He decided to stop by.

The Morrison home hadn't changed a bit since he last saw it. He reined up out front and tied his horse. It was getting dusky dark when he knocked on the door, half expecting Mary Ann to open the door to greet him. Instead, John Morrison opened the door.

Surprise spread all over the farmer's face when recognition finally found a home.

"Jubal Hawk! What a surprise."

"Is Mary Ann here?" Jubal asked.

"Mary Ann? Why... no, she's at her own home over in Lenoir City. Oh, I reckon you didn't know she was married, did you?"

It was Jubal's turn to be surprised—and he was.

"No, sir, I hadn't heard that."

"Who is it, John?" a woman's voice called from another room.

"It's Jubal Hawk. You remember Jubal."

Mrs. Morrison appeared, wiping her hands on an apron. She approached the front door with a big smile.

"Of course I do! How are you, Jubal?"

"I'm fine, Mrs. Morrison, ma'am. I just got home and stopped by to say hello to Mary Ann. I didn't know she was married. Reckon I better be going."

"Nonsense! We were just about to sit down to supper. Will you join us?"

"No, ma'am, I couldn't."

"Of course you could! I won't take no for an answer. Come on in," she said, grasping his arm and pulling him into the house. "We don't get to see Mary Ann near enough, she's so busy. They have a large plantation just outside Lenoir City."

"Who did she marry?" Jubal asked.

"Wayne Lenoir. Did you know him? He's about your age. He's the oldest son of Isaac Lenoir, the founder of Sweetwater."

"No, ma'am, I didn't know him," Jubal said.

"Pull out a chair and sit down," Mr. Morrison invited, motioning to a chair at the dining table.

"I'm afraid all we're having is rabbit stew and corn bread," Mrs. Morrison said, setting another plate and silverware in front of him. "Times have been hard since the war."

"That's one of my favorite meals," he lied.

But he ate like a starving man and found the food delicious. He complimented Mrs. Morrison several times on the meal.

"I was shore sorry to hear about your pa," Mr. Morrison said around a mouthful of buttered cornbread and sorghum molasses.

"Thank you, sir. I hear there's quite a bit of that sort of stuff going on around here."

"Yes, some folks just can't accept that the war is finally over. I hear they hung your father and burned you out, too."

"Yes, sir, and stole our horse herd while they were at it."

"Any idea who did it?"

"Not yet, but I'm sure gonna find out. The so-called sheriff don't seem interested in doing anything about it."

"Oh, I figure he knows who done it, alright, but knowing and doing something about it is another thing. He's as worthless as tits on a boar hog."

"JOHN!" Mrs. Morrison said loudly. "Watch your language!"

"Well, the truth's the truth," he insisted.

"Well, even if it is, that doesn't give you an excuse to use that kind of language in this house."

Mr. Morrison seemed adequately reprimanded and lifted a one-sided grin and a wink at Jubal.

"I really enjoyed the meal, Mrs. Morrison," Jubal said, pushing up from his chair. "Give Mary Ann my congratulations when you see her and tell her I wish her much happiness."

"I will do that, Jubal. Thank you for stopping by. Do it again soon."

It was pitch dark when he left the Morrison home. He short-loped his buckskin most of the way back home. Wash was nowhere in sight when he arrived, so he unsaddled Buck and watered him from the water trough. He unrolled his bedroll and spread it beside the water trough on the ground—he was used to sleeping on the ground—he had done it for the last five years.

Wash woke him just after first light with a wide smile.

"You look awfully happy this morning," Jubal greeted him, sloshing water from the water trough on his whiskered face and scrubbing it with his hands.

"Come on, we having squirrel for breakfast," the big black man told him.

"How'd you manage to catch a squirrel?" Jubal asked.

"A man can do what a man's gotta do when he has to," Wash answered.

Jubal followed his friend into the bushes where he found a fire going in front of a make-do lean-to shelter.

"Have a seat," Wash invited.

Jubal sat down on a large log near the campfire. Wash handed him a roasted squirrel leg with steam still coming from it.

Jubal took it, juggled it a few times because it was so hot, and took a testing bite. He found it delicious, ate every bite, and licked the bone.

"I wasn't able to get any supplies," he explained to his friend. "Seems my Confederate money's no good any more."

"Don't matter none," Wash told him. "I been doing just fine for a spell. I be just fine."

"I'm gonna ride over to Pigeon Forge and check on my folks, but I'll be back and we'll start building another house."

"I'll be watchin' fer you, Master Jubal, sir. Yes, sir, I shore will."

CHAPTER II

Pigeon Forge, Tennessee was a mountain community located in a narrow valley tucked between two large mountain ranges. It was several days' ride to the northeast near the Great Smokey Mountains. Arthur and Aubrey Bilbrey had a nice home built on the side of a mountain just west of town overlooking Clear Fork Creek down below. Arthur was a lumberjack who worked for a local lumber mill. Jubal had only been to their home once when he was a young boy.

Buck struggled up the well-worn road to the sprawling, slat cedar house that hugged the side of the mountain. A wide front porch stretched the entire length of the house. A comfortable-looking cedar porch swing hung from chains suspended from the ceiling. He reined up and tied his horse to a hitching rail in front of the house.

"Hello, the house!" he called loudly.

The front door suddenly burst open and his little brother leaped from the porch to greet him—only he wasn't so little any more. The strapping boy stood near as tall as his own six feet. His long, straw-colored hair matched Jubal's. His younger brother slammed into Jubal's open arms.

"When did you get home, Jubal? We sure missed you!"

"I missed you too, Jason. You're all growed up. What are you? Nineteen now?"

"Yep."

Another flying body crashed into him. It was a beautiful blond haired young lady with the same mischievous smile he remembered—a smile that would light up any room as bright as the morning sun.

"This can't possibly be that little pig-tailed sister of mine?"

"I'm afraid so," she laughed. "We missed you, Jubal."

"I know. I'm sorry, little sis. I wish I had been here."

Tears escaped her eyes and she nodded her head, unable to speak.

"JUBAL!" a woman's familiar voice screamed.

He swung a look. His mother stood on the front porch with her arms open wide. He hurried to fill them. They hugged. She clung to him and they cried together for a long time before she would let him go.

When he looked again the front porch was half-filled with folks; most of them he didn't know and had never seen before. It took awhile for him to meet all of them and he couldn't have remembered their names if his life depended on it.

Arthur Bilbrey shook his hand and lifted a one-sided grin. He was big—bigger even than Jubal; a mountain of a man who must have weighed three hundred and towered well over six feet.

"Good to have you home, Jubal," he said.

"Thanks, Arthur. Believe me, it's good to be home. It was mighty good of you to take my family in like you did. We'll be rebuilding the house and getting them out of your hair before long."

"No hurry, we're enjoying having them; they're family."

"Mighty decent of you," Jubal told him, releasing his hand.

"Come on inside, we've got a pot of coffee on."

"Now that's an invite I can't refuse," Jubal said.

Together they went inside and sat at a huge, polished cedar table.

Aubrey brought cups and a pot of coffee. They all sat around the table and visited for the next hour or more.

"Any word yet on who raided your home and hung your father?" Arthur asked.

"Not yet, but I'll find out if I have to turn over every rock in Tennessee," Jubal assured him.

"Think it might be a bunch of Yankee sympathizers out for revenge?"

"Maybe, we'll find out," Jubal told him.

Later, they all enjoyed a supper of cured ham, potato salad, and corn on the cob. They visited until late and bedded down on quilt pallets scattered all over the house.

The next day Jubal and his mother walked out to the front porch with their cups of coffee and sat in the porch swing together.

"I stopped by the bank in Sweetwater," Jubal told her. "Mr. Stringfellow said you drew all of our money out and sold Pa's stock in the bank. How we fixed for money?"

"Yes, I felt like we would need the money more than we needed stock in the bank. I have it all in a satchel under the bed. I haven't counted it, but it looks like an awful lot to me."

"What do you think we ought to do, Ma?" he asked.

"You are the head of the family now, Jubal. What do you think? We'll do whatever you think best."

"I've been giving it lots of thought. We've got clear title to over five hundred acres of the best land in Monroe County. There ain't better horse-raising land anywhere. Somewhere, we've got a herd of over a hundred head of prime horses. I aim to find them and see the ones that stole them are punished."

"I tried to talk with the sheriff, but he paid me no mind. He laughed in my face."

"We'll deal with the sheriff when the time comes. Right now we need to rebuild our house and horse barns and get our family back together again. Reckon you and Mary Lou could stay here a while longer while me and Jason set to work building a house?"

"They said we could stay as long as we needed to."

"Good. Then me and Jason will head out tomorrow and get started. We'll come for you as soon as we can."

Arthur knew where they could find a good riding horse for Jason. He went with Jubal and Jason to pick one out. Jason selected a red sorrel with a blaze face and two white stockings. They bought a new saddle and rigging at the same place. Jubal also bought Jason a Remington, double-barrel shotgun with a twelve inch barrel and a saddle holster to carry it in. He purchased six boxes of double-aught shells for it. He also bought Jason a ground sheet and a bedroll to carry behind his new saddle. He purchased two new Henry rifles and saddle scabbards for them. Jubal carried the same sidearm he had used during the later part of the war. It was a 1865 Navy pistol that used a self-contained cartridge. It had served him well and he had become quite proficient at drawing and firing the weapon. Jason rode tall in the saddle as they rode side by side back to the Bilbrey house to say goodbye.

Arthur eyed all the hardware on their saddles as they rode up and tied their horses.

"Expecting trouble?" he asked.

"Trouble's already found us," Jubal replied. "It's fell on us to meet it face to face."

After the *goodbyes* were all said, Jubal and Jason headed for home. They rode proudly side by side. Jubal didn't remember ever feeling prouder.

"I want to swing by Madisonville on the way home," Jubal told his younger brother. "It's not far out of our way."

They arrived in the county seat of Monroe County at mid-morning of the third day after leaving Pigeon Forge. Monroe County was mostly mountainous country and heavily wooded; one of only a handful of areas of the county with large, clear mountain valleys was the land belonging to the Hawk family. They reined up in front of the county courthouse.

"Can I help you, sir?" a heavy-set lady asked as he entered the office.

"Yes, ma'am. I'm Jubal Hawk. We own five hundred acres over by Sweetwater. I just got back from the war and would like to check on our taxes."

The lady had to check several large books before she returned.

"Yes, sir, I'm afraid your taxes for that five hundred acres are overdue. In fact, it has already been placed for auction to the highest bidder."

The news gave birth to a knot in the pit of his stomach.

Their land? Up for bid to the highest bidder? How could that be?

"My father was murdered and my mother didn't know nothing about the taxes. Can't I pay the back taxes and avoid the auction? Isn't there some kind of time limit I have to pay the taxes and redeem our land?"

"Well, yes. Normally, we have to wait five years before we are allowed to seize the property for non-payment of taxes, but there are exceptions made if a judge signs off on it. It seems Judge Robert Little made an exception in this case because we already have a party interested in the land."

"And who is that party that's *interested* in our land?"

"Let me look. Yes, here it is, it's Colonel John T. Jessup."

"How much are my taxes?"

"With all penalties and interest, they come to eighty-seven dollars."

He counted out the amount and threw it down on the counter.

"But sir, I have already explained that we cannot accept the payment since Judge Little has signed a waiver."

"I want a receipt for my taxes and I want it right now!" I will bring you a release signed by the judge. Where can I find this Judge Little?"

"His office is right down the hall."

Jubal stalked out of the clerk's office and headed down the hall. Judge Little's name was on a frosted glass door. He opened the door and pushed inside.

"I'd like to see Judge Little," he told the woman behind a desk.

"I'm sorry, sir," she said. "He's busy. Maybe you could make an appointment for later in the week."

Without another word Jubal turned and opened the only other door in the room. A short, sweaty, heavy-set fellow with balding hair sat behind a large desk smoking a fat cigar. Another fellow sat on the front side of the desk. The cigar-smoker jerked a look.

"What's the meaning of you barging in here unannounced?" he demanded in an angry voice.

Jubal strode around the desk and grabbed the cigar from the judge's mouth. He crushed it in a fist.

"My name's Jubal Hawk. You and Colonel Jessup are trying to steal my land. I won't stand for it. I want a signed statement by you revoking the exception you made on my land and I want it *right now!*"

"You can't do this! I'll have you arrested!"

Jubal grabbed a handful of shirt and lifted the fat man from his chair. He lowered his face to within an inch of the judge's face. The next words pushed between clenched teeth.

"You do and I'll come back and cram that fat cigar down your throat. *Nobody's* gonna steal my land! *Nobody!* Am I making myself clear?"

The frightened judge nodded his head and scribbled words on a paper revoking the exception he had signed.

"Sign it and date it," Jubal demanded.

With the paper in hand, he returned to the clerk's office and showed her the paper.

"Now cancel that auction and mark my taxes paid in full. I want to see it in the book."

The frightened lady did as he demanded and showed him the notation in the records book. He folded the paper the judge signed and put it in his pocked as he left the courthouse.

"Everything alright?" Jason asked.

"It is now," Jubal said, toeing a stirrup and swinging into the saddle. "Let's ride."

CHAPTER III

Jubal rode into Lenoir City the next day after arriving back home. He left Jason with Wash to watch after their land.

He went directly to the lumberyard when he arrived in Lenoir City.

"Who's the best carpenter in Lenoir City?" he asked the manager of the lumberyard.

"That would be Ike Smally," the manager said without hesitation.

"Can he build a nice house?"

"He can build whatever you want."

"Where can I find him?"

"He lives a couple of streets over on Walnut Street. It's a big white house with green shutters. You can't miss it."

"If he takes the job we'll be needing all the materials. Can I set up an account for him to get what he needs? I'll put enough in escrow to cover it. Can you make arrangements to deliver the materials to the job site?"

"Be glad to. Where will you be building?"

"Twelve miles southwest of Sweetwater on the east fork of the Little Tennessee River. It's the only open valley for miles. We've got a horse ranch there. My name's Jubal Hawk."

"After you make your deal with Ike, stop back by and we'll make the arrangements."

"I'll be back," Jubal said, turning and leaving the store.

He found the house without difficulty and knocked on the door. A middle-age fellow with a friendly looking face opened the door.

"Looking for Ike Smally."

"You found him," the man said, sticking out his hand.

They shared a firm handshake.

"My name's Jubal Hawk. The fellow down at the lumberyard said you could build anything. Was he lying to me?"

"Mister, I could have built the Egyptian pyramids if it hadn't been so far to swim."

Jubal laughed and patted the fellow on the shoulder.

"Got a job for you, Ike."

Over a few cups of coffee at Ike's kitchen table, the carpenter listened to Jubal's ideas and sketched out rough plans for the house Jubal wanted.

"I made arrangements with the lumber yard to deliver whatever you needed. Just give him a list of the materials you'll need.

"I could use a helper for a job that big," Ike told him.

"Hire whoever you want. What will it cost me for a job like this?"

"I charge three dollars a day. My helper gets half that much."

"You got a deal," Jubal said, extending his hand to seal the bargain. "When can you start?"

"We'll be there in three days. I'll make the arrangement for the material to be delivered."

Jubal left Lenoir City feeling good.

True to his word, Ike Smally and his helper, a man named Dan Engles, arrived on the third day after Jubal returned from Lenoir City. They set up tents as temporary shelters during construction.

With them, came three wagonloads of lumber and building materials. Before nightfall they had the perimeters of the new house staked out and digging for the foundation was underway. Wash and Jason helped with the digging. Jubal left for Sweetwater to pick up food supplies.

He stopped first at the livery stable with the intention of buying a team of horses and a new wagon. Jake Foley, the blacksmith and livery owner, had been a friend of the Hawk family for years. He was shoeing a bay mare when Jubal reined up.

"Morning, Jake," he greeted their old friend.

The smithy looked up from his task with several horseshoe nails protruding from his lips. He stood upright and removed the nails before returning the greeting.

"Jubal Hawk! Well I declare, I almost didn't recognize you. You've grown a right smart since I seen you last."

"It's been awhile," Jubal acknowledged.

"Somebody said they saw you in town a few days back. You home for good?"

"Yep, we're rebuilding our house the *night-riders* burned down after they hung my pa."

"Yeah, them varmints been wreaking havoc all over this whole area lately."

"Know anybody that rides a big black and white pinto?"

Jake slanted a questioning look at him before answering.

"Why you asking?"

"One of the *night-riders* that hung my father and burned us out rode a big black and white pinto."

"The only pinto I know about in these parts belongs to Vance Slater. He's Colonel Jessup's foreman. Be right careful around Slater, Jubal, he's mean as a sidewinder."

"Jessup, again. I've been hearing that name pop up a lot lately. What do you know about this *Jessup* fellow?"

"Not much. He moved to Monroe County a couple years ago. He seems to have lots of money, but nobody seems to know where he got it. He's got a big spread down river from your place along the Little Tennessee.

"He runs a lot of horses. I ain't been out there but once. The Colonel's somewhat of a *loner,* he don't get out a lot. He's got more horse wranglers than normal for a spread his size."

"Maybe I ought to go have a talk with this *Vance Slater."*

"I wouldn't do that if I was you. From what I've seen he's poison mean. The men that work for the Colonel ain't normal wranglers—they're *fighting men."*

"Much obliged for the information. By the way, I'm needing a good team and a wagon; got anything like that?"

"If I ain't I need to get out of this business. Walk on back to the corral out back and pick out what looks good to you."

Jubal dismounted and walked to a large corral behind the livery and blacksmith shop. He propped a booted foot on the bottom rail of the corral and studied the twenty or so horses milling around inside.

Two big matching bays caught his eye. They stood at least seventeen hands and Jubal guessed them to weigh fourteen to sixteen hundred pounds. He could tell by the slick and shiny color of their coats that they were healthy.

He climbed the fence and moved slowly through the horse herd until his arm circled one of the bays. He pried open its mouth and examined its teeth. He guessed the horse to be around six years old. Lifting a fore foot, he examined the bare hoof and found it healthy. He caught the matching horse and found it identical to the first.

Jake walked up to the corral fence as Jubal dropped the hoof of the bay. The livery owner lifted a one-sided grin.

"I knew before I come back you'd pick them two bays. They're the best two horses in the corral. Your pappy trained you well."

"How much?"

"I'll take a hundred apiece for them."

Jubal shook his head.

"I'll give eighty."

Jake studied on it for a long minute.

"Make it ninety and you've got a deal."

"I'll give ninety apiece if you'll throw in a set of harness."

"Deal."

"Now I need a work wagon."

"Got four brand new Nashville three-board wagons sitting back yonder in the shed."

"What you asking for them?"

"Two hundred-fifty apiece. One or all of them."

"Just one for now."

Jubal counted out four hundred-thirty dollars into Jake's open hand.

"Hitch 'em up to a wagon for me. I'll be back in an hour."

"You got it. They'll be ready."

CHAPTER IV

Jubal climbed into his saddle and rode to the Sweetwater General Store. Carl Hamburg looked up from stocking a shelf and nodded.

"I need two sets of clothes from the skin out, nothing fancy, just plain working clothes, and boots. I'll keep Confederate hat. Got kinda attached to it."

"You do remember I don't take Confederate money," the store owner told him.

"I remember."

Jubal selected the boots and tried them on. Mr. Hamburg gathered the items he ordered and laid them on the counter—and waited. Jubal laid a twenty dollar gold coin on the counter.

"Will that cover it?" he asked.

"Oh, yeah. You've got change coming."

"Is there someplace I can change clothes?" Jubal handed the store owner a long list of supplies. "I'll be back shortly to load them in my wagon."

"They'll be ready and waiting. You're welcome to use the storeroom right back yonder to change your clothes."

Jubal gathered his purchases and found the storeroom. He shed the ragged Confederate Cavalry uniform and climbed into his new civilian clothes. On the way out he bought a new gun belt and open holster for his Navy model handgun. He strapped the gun belt around his waist and tied the tie-down to his right leg. He checked to make sure his gun was loaded before stepping out onto the street.

On the way to the livery he stopped by the barber shop. He had known Ray Muse, the barber, for as long as he could remember.

"Howdy, Jubal!" the barber greeted. "I heard you were back. Good to have you home."

"Howdy, Ray. It's good to be back too. I need a shave and haircut."

"Sit down. We'll see what we can do to make you look like the Jubal Hawk I remember."

They visited as the barber worked. When he finished he removed the big striped cloth and shook the hair from it. Jubal looked in the big mirror behind the barber chair.

He had worn a beard so long he hardly recognized the face staring back at him. It was a hard-set face, made hard by witnessing too many men dying too young—many by his own hand. He saw a face with lake-blue eyes and a square jaw. His straw-colored hair barely touched his collar.

He handed the barber a dollar.

"Much obliged, Ray."

"Come again, Jubal."

His team of horses was hitched to his new wagon and waiting when he arrived at the livery. He tied Buck behind the wagon and headed back to the store to pick up the supplies he had ordered earlier.

He loaded the supplies into the new wagon and filled the rest of the space with sacks of feed for their horses.

While loading the feed, two hard-looking strangers sauntered up, leaned against the posts in front of the store, and eyed him closely.

One was a tall, lanky fellow with pock marks on his face. He had an ugly knife scar from his cheek to his neck and crooked teeth. He wore a Navy model 1865 pistol in an open holster similar to Jubal's. He judged the man to be a real hard case and looked like trouble with a capital T.

The second fellow was short and stocky and carried a Henry rifle tucked into the crook of his arm.

"A fellow over in the saloon said you was a *Johnny Reb.* Is that true?"

Jubal set the sack of feed in his wagon and slanted a look at the tall fellow who asked the question.

Several passersby heard the loud, angry voice and stopped to listen. Jubal noticed that one of them was the banker, Mr. Stringfellow.

"I fought for the Confederacy, if that's what you're asking. You got a problem with that?"

"Yeah, I got a problem with that! We don't like *stinking yellow-belly Rebs* in these parts. We hang 'em from the nearest tree!"

"Who's *we*? You one of them *night-riders* I been hearing about that's so scared you hide your face under a toe-sack?

"I ain't scared of nothing or nobody!"

"Mister, the war's over. You best let it lay. I ain't looking for trouble."

"Besides being a *yella-belly Reb,* I say you're a dirty, rotten, *coward*! You're wearing a gun. I'm calling you out!" the man shouted. "Either tuck your tail and run or slap leather!"

Jubal flicked a quick look at the man's companion.

"Are you part of this?" he asked.

"I'm with him," the shorter man answered, spitting a long stream of tobacco juice in Jubal's direction.

"Then you'll die with him," Jubal squeezed the words between clenched teeth. He squared around to face the two troublemakers.

Jubal's hand settled comfortably just below the butt of his pistol. He fixed an unwavering stare at the eyes of Scarface.

He'll most likely be the faster of the two. I'll have to take him first and hope I have enough time to deal with the one with the rifle.

"Do what you think you gotta do," Jubal told the man. "It's your call."

Scarface hesitated for a short moment in time. Suddenly his lips clamped together in sheer hatred and determination. His right hand clawed for the pistol on his hip.

Jubal purposely waited until his opponent's pistol was half-way out of its holster before his hand swept the .36 caliber Navy Colt from his own holster. His thumb raked back the hammer as his weapon cleared the holster. As the Colt rose to the target he feathered the trigger.

The blast rocked his hand upward. The jarring sensation journeyed up his arm to his shoulder. He saw a thumb-size hole suddenly appear in the center of his opponent's chest. A thin spray of crimson squirted from the hole. Scarface's shot punched a harmless gouge in the dirt in front of his own feet.

Immediately Jubal swung the nose of his Colt toward the one with the rifle. As he did, he swept the hammer of his Colt back a second time. The man with the rifle was swinging it toward Jubal. Instinctively, Jubal twisted his body to his left as the rifle exploded. The .44 slug swished past his chest and buried into the side board of his wagon.

He felt his Colt explode a second time. The short rifleman suddenly dropped his rifle and staggered two steps backward in an awkward dance of death. His legs buckled under him and he collapsed in the dirt beside his dead companion.

Jubal stepped forward and kicked Scarface's pistol out of reach in case he was only wounded. Squatting beside the attackers, he felt their necks for a pulse. He needn't have worried—both men were stone-cold dead.

Jubal rose and was holstering his Colt when he felt the hard press of something in the small of his back.

"I'll take that gun, *Reb*!" a voice from behind him said.

Jubal twisted a look over his shoulder—it was the sheriff and a large man with a deputy sheriff's badge pinned on his vest. The sheriff had a sawed-off, double-barrel shotgun pressed against his back.

"You're under arrest, *Reb*! You just killed two men," the lawman snarled, reaching and removing Jubal's Colt from his holster.

"It was self-defense. He drew first."

"You gonna walk down the street to my jail or do I drag you?"

"Ask any of these folks, they'll tell you it was self-defense," Jubal told the lawman.

"They'll have a chance to tell their story at the trial, now *move!*"

Jubal turned a look at the banker and the storekeeper. Jake Foley was also there along with a dozen others.

"You men saw what happened. Tell him!"

"He's right, Sheriff. The others drew first," Mr. Stringfellow said.

"I saw it all, Sheriff," the store owner agreed. "This man didn't want the fight. The others prodded him into it. It was clearly self-defense."

"Save it for the trial," the sheriff told them as he jammed the nose of the shotgun into Jubal's back. "Now move or I swear I'll kill you right here!"

"Jake, will you see that my wagonload of supplies and my horse get to the ranch? Tell my brother what happened."

"I'll take care of it myself, Jubal," the liveryman said.

* * *

The small jail cell was completely empty except for a rock slab cot built into one of the side walls. There was no window; the only way in or out was the heavy wood slab door that opened into the sheriff's office.

Jubal sat on the rock cot and tried to analyze his situation.

The sheriff had no call to arrest me. The shooting was self-defense without question. There were at least a dozen witnesses that saw it.

My problem is the sheriff's the law in Sweetwater. He can do pretty much whatever he wants to do. Looks like his intention is to hold me until a trial can be arranged and no telling how long that will take. Looks like I'm in a real pickle.

Time passed slowly. Darkness filtered through the small crack underneath the wooden door. He heard comings and goings in the sheriff's office, but wasn't able to make out any of their conversation.

Sometime after dark the heavy door suddenly opened. Three hooded men with toe- sacks over their heads entered his cell. He sensed something bad was about to happen and backed up against the back wall of the tiny cell.

All three hooded men rushed him at the same time. He managed to get in a couple of good licks before they overpowered him and pinned him to the floor. They roughly tied his hands behind his back with a short length of rope.

He lay there on his stomach on the cold rock floor with all three men standing around him. One of them wore a pair of silver spurs with a five-pointed star rowel. Suddenly the one with the spurs lashed out with a booted foot. The blow struck him in his side. He heard the snap of bone and knew the blow had broken his rib. Excruciating pain shot through his entire body. The other two joined the first in kicking him. How long he was able to endure before the sanctuary of unconsciousness brought welcome relief, he didn't know.

Sometime later he awoke. It was pitch black in his tiny cell. Pain like he had never known before racked every inch of his body. He tried to lick his lips, but they were split, bruised, and bleeding. The acrid taste of his own blood filled his mouth. He lay in a fetal position on the rock floor. The tiny jail cell swirled and spun. He slipped in and out of consciousness. He clamped his lips tightly together in an unsuccessful effort to stifle the uncontrollable moans that erupted from deep inside. Once, during a period of consciousness, he felt a wet, sticky substance where his bruised face lay on the floor—it was a puddle of his own blood.

Somehow he made it through the long and agonizing night. A thin hint of light crept underneath the wooden door and slowly swallowed up the darkness. He managed to pry open his eyes and saw the dark puddle of his own blood underneath his face. He tried to move. Excruciating pain shot through his head. He drew a deep breath, gritted his teeth, and slowly, painfully, rolled over onto his back.

He heard a key turn in a lock and the heavy wooden door to his cell swung open. The burly deputy sheriff he remembered from earlier stepped into the cell carrying two wooden buckets. He set the buckets on the floor beside Jubal.

"Did you sleep good, *Reb?*" the deputy asked, chuckling out loud. "I brought you some water and a slop bucket. Make yourself at home, looks like you're gonna be with us awhile."

The deputy left the cell and locked the door.

It was a struggle, but he finally managed to reach the water bucket. He splashed several handfuls onto his face. The blood had dried and was hard to get off. He cupped a handful into his open mouth before settling his head back onto the floor.

Loud voices from the outer office reached his hearing— one of them sounded like Jason, his younger brother.

"I want to see my brother!" the voice demanded.

The heavy door finally opened. Jason and Marvin Stringfellow hurried past the deputy and knelt beside Jubal with deep concern written on their faces.

"What happened here?" the banker demanded. "This man has been beaten half to death."

The deputy shrugged his shoulders, unconcerned.

"He must have tripped and fell against the bunk of something. He was fine when we locked him up."

"Well, he's not fine now. Jason, run and get the doctor as fast as you can and bring him back here with you. Your brother needs medical help."

Jason immediately rose and hurried out.

"This is outrageous!" the banker shouted. "This man shouldn't even be in jail. He did absolutely nothing wrong. Where's the sheriff? I want to see the sheriff!"

"He don't come in until noon or so."

"Go get him! He's got some explaining to do," the banker demanded. "I want to see him and I want to see him right now!"

"I can't do that. I'm not allowed to leave the office when we've got a prisoner in jail."

"Then lock the door and go get him. I'm staying with Jubal Hawk until we get this straightened out."

The deputy refused to leave, but he sent someone to get the sheriff in view of the banker's demands.

Doctor Wilson arrived and quickly examined Jubal with concern reflected on his face. He said Jubal had at least two broken ribs, maybe more, and a concussion in the head from the beating he endured. His face was cut and swollen almost beyond recognition.

"This man's fortunate to be alive," the doctor said. "In all my years of practice I don't recall anyone being beaten this bad."

Marvin Stringfellow called Jason aside. He withdrew a piece of paper and a pencil from an inside pocket of his suit jacket. He scribbled something on it, folded it, and handed it to Jason.

"Jason, I want you to ride to Lenoir City as quickly as you can. Find Wade Henson's office. He's the best attorney in this part of Tennessee. Tell him I sent for him and that he's to come at once. Give him this note. Can you do this for your brother?"

"Yes, sir."

Jason kicked on the wooden door until the deputy opened it and let him out. The deputy then re-locked the door with the banker and doctor inside.

Doctor Wilson was wrapping a tight bandage around Jubal's broken ribs when the door opened and Sheriff Bullock walked in. "The deputy says there's a problem with the prisoner. What's wrong with him?'

"Somebody's beat this man half to death," the banker said angrily. "That's what's wrong with him! I'm a member of the town council and I promise you we are gonna find out who done this!"

"There was nothing wrong with him when we locked him up yesterday. He must have done this to himself."

"Nonsense! That's impossible! I want to know who did this and I want to know right now!"

"Three men," Jubal mumbled through bruised, cut, and swollen lips. They wore toe-sack hoods."

"Deuce!" the sheriff hollered to his deputy. "Get in here!"

The big deputy hurried through the door at the tone of the sheriff's voice.

"Did you leave the jail unattended at any time last night?"

The deputy hesitated, shifting nervously from one foot to the other. His frightened look darted from the sheriff to the banker and back again.

"I just ran up to the café to get a bite to eat for supper, that's all. I wasn't gone but a few minutes."

"You know good and well that's against my rules! I've told you time and again, you *never* leave the jail unattended when you've got a prisoner. You've caused a big ruckus. Turn in your badge, you're fired!"

"But—but you said . . . ."

Sheriff Bullock abruptly interrupted his deputy.

"But while you were gone somebody helped themselves to the key and beat the prisoner up. Turn in your badge—you're through!"

"But you told me . . ."

"Shut your mouth!" the sheriff interrupted the deputy again. "Don't say another word!"

The sheriff ripped the deputy sheriff badge from the deputy's chest and threw it on the floor.

"Get outta my sight! Does that satisfy you *Stringfellow?*" the sheriff asked.

"It's a start, but frankly, the real problem isn't your deputy, it's you! What have you done to find these hooded *night-riders* and bring them to justice? They hung one of Sweetwater's most outstanding citizens and burned his house to the ground. It's been over three months and I haven't seen one single arrest."

"Nobody knows who they are or even if they actually exist or not. I can't run around looking for someone when I don't know who I'm looking for."

"Well, you can start by releasing Jubal Hawk. You and I both know he was acting in self-defense. At least a dozen Sweetwater citizens will testify those two men started the fight and drew first."

"I can't do that. He gunned down two men like dogs. He's gonna stand trial for that. If it turns out like you say, that's all well and good. My duty was to arrest him and hold him for trial."

"It was *also* your duty to protect him while he is in your custody and you failed miserably. I'm going to see that you answer for that in front of the town council."

"Well, you do what you gotta do and I'll do the same," the sheriff said. "The judge will be here the day after tomorrow, until then he'll stay locked up in jail."

Jubal was mostly awake and heard the discussion between the sheriff and banker. He wasn't convinced that the sheriff didn't have something to do with his beating; maybe he didn't actually take part himself, but knew it was going to happen and allowed it.

It was an old score that he would settle when the time was right.

The day passed agonizingly slow. The doctor had to leave to tend to other patients, but promised to return the following day to change the bandages. The banker also had to leave, but promised to return later that afternoon after the bank closed.

Jason returned just before sundown with a well-dressed man. Jason introduced him as Wade Henson, an attorney at law from Lenoir City. They exchanged handshakes as Jubal sized up the man. He was tall and well groomed. He wore a gray business suit that was obviously tailor-made and very expensive. He had coal-black hair that was slicked back. A pleasant smile set Jubal at ease. He decided right off that Wade Henson was a man to be trusted.

"Tell me exactly what happened as well as you remember. Leave nothing out. Any small detail might be the very thing we need to make this go away."

Jubal related the events leading up to the shooting and his arrest. The attorney listened intently and took notes as Jubal talked.

"As near as you can remember, tell me who was there and saw what happened," the attorney requested.

"Marvin Stringfellow, of course; Jesse Hamburg, he owns the general store; Jake Foley, the blacksmith and owner of the livery; Mrs. Rawlings, she owns a ladies dress shop next door to the general store; Ray Muse, the barber, and several others I didn't recognize."

"According to the sheriff, the judge will be in town the day after tomorrow, so I've got to get moving. I want to take a deposition from everybody who was there and saw what happened. I will need you to testify, so you need to get all the rest you can between now and the trial."

"I'll be okay," Jubal said. "I can testify."

"I'll be back tomorrow and give you an update. I'll be staying in the hotel until this is over," the attorney told him. "If you need me for anything, just send word."

The attorney left, but Jason stayed with his brother.

"I'm gonna spend the night to make sure nothing happens to you tonight," his brother said.

Jubal nodded his head.

"Help me up onto the cot," Jubal asked.

Jason helped his brother onto the rock cot. It was as hard as the floor, but not as dirty.

Jason sat down on the floor with his back against the side of the cot. They talked for awhile until Jubal drifted off to sleep.

It was a long and uncomfortable night, but morning finally arrived. Doctor Wilson came to check on his patient and change the bandages.

"I'm gonna run down to the café and get him some breakfast while you're here," Jason said.

"Don't worry, I will stay until you get back," the doctor said.

Jason returned shortly with a pot of coffee, cups, and a tray holding a breakfast of biscuits and flour gravy with sliced ham on the side.

It hurt terribly to chew, but Jubal ate like a starving man. What he couldn't eat, Jason finished off. Just before noon, Wade Henson arrived with a smile on his face.

"Good news," the attorney told them. "I've got depositions from eight local citizens who will testify they saw everything that happened. They will swear the other man drew first and that you acted in self-defense. The sheriff had absolutely no grounds to arrest you, so, relax, this will all be over tomorrow."

"I'll relax when this is over and done," Jubal said.

CHAPTER V

The door to Jubal's cell swung open. The sheriff and a new deputy Jubal hadn't seen before entered carrying handcuffs and leg irons. Sheriff Bullock held his gun on Jubal and Jason while the deputy locked the irons in place.

"Let's go," the sheriff ordered.

The leg irons were connected by a short length of chain making it difficult for Jubal to walk. He had to shuffle his feet along the floor in baby-like steps.

The trial was to be held in the churchhouse since it was the largest building in Sweetwater. Jubal had trouble lifting his feet to climb the steps, so the sheriff and the deputy got on either side and lifted him onto the porch.

The church building was jam-packed. Others who couldn't find a seat stood against the inside wall. The sheriff and his deputy led Jubal down the aisle to a straight-back chair beside his attorney, Wade Henson.

A woman Jubal recognized as the clerk he had met earlier in the county courthouse in Madisonville regarding his taxes sat at a small table with a pad of paper in front of her.

I sure hope it ain't the same judge I threatened to make eat his cigar. If it is I'm in more trouble than I thought.

The court clerk stood and said loudly.

"All rise. County Judge Robert Little presiding."

Oh me, Jubal thought, dropping his head. *This ain't gonna go well, I can feel it.*

A door opened at the side of the small platform and the fat little judge from Madisonville shuffled in wearing a black robe. He sat down in a leather-covered, high-backed chair facing the audience.

"You may be seated," the clerk announced. "Case number eight, Monroe County, Tennessee versus Mr. Jubal Hawk."

The judge looked directly at Jubal and spoke. "Mr. Hawk, we meet again. Jubal Hawk, you are charged with two counts of first degree murder in the deaths of Troy Head and Colby Middleton. How do you plead?"

Wade Henson stood.

"Your Honor, I'm Wade Henson, attorney at law from Lenoir City. I am representing Mr. Hawk. He pleads *not guilty.* Also, my client has a right to a jury trial. I request that a jury be selected."

"Request denied," the judge said sternly. "I will try this case."

"But Your Honor . . ." Jubal's attorney objected.

"Sit down, Mr. Henson. Your request has been *denied!*"

"You can't do that!" Wade Henson said loudly. "This man has a constitutional right to a trial by a jury of his peers. I insist on exercising that right!"

"Your objection will be noted for the record, however, there will be *no jury* called in this case. Now sit down before I hold you in contempt! I understand Sheriff Bullock will be prosecuting the case. Is that true?"

"Yes, sir," the sheriff said, rising to his feet and stepping forward.

"Then call your first witness."

"I call Benny Sand."

A tall, lanky cowboy stood to his feet near the back of the building and made his way down the aisle to the witness chair in the front of the room. Once the cowboy stood in front of the witness chair the county clerk held a Bible out to him.

"Place your left hand on the Bible and raise your right hand. Do you swear the testimony you are about to give in this case is the truth, the whole truth, and nothing but the truth so help you God?"

"Yeah, I do," the cowboy answered.

"Tell the court your name," the sheriff said.

"Benny Sand."

"Did you witness a gunfight in front of the Sweetwater General Store?"

"Yep, shore did."

"Is one of the men involved in that gunfight in the courtroom today?"

"Yep, sitting right over there in chains."

"Tell the court what you saw."

"I saw that fellow gun down two of my friends, Troy Head and Colby Middleton. He drew down on them for no reason. They didn't stand a chance."

"Are you saying he's the one that started the fight?"

"I shore am. They both tried to settle the argument without a fight, but he just kept pushing it."

"Your witness," the sheriff said, twisting a smirk as he sat down.

Jubal's attorney rose and walked over to stand directly in front of the witness.

"What do you do for a living, Mr. Sand?"

"I'm a horse wrangler."

"Are you presently employed?"

"Yep."

"And where do you work?"

"I work for Colonel Jessup on the Box J Ranch."

"Did Troy Head and Colby Middleton also work for this Colonel Jessup?"

"Yeah, we worked together."

"In fact, the three of you were drinking together the day of the shooting weren't you?"

"Yeah, so what?"

"The three of you palled around together, didn't you?"

"Yep, we were friends."

"Did either you or your two *friends* serve in the military during the war?"

"Now just hold on right there!" Sheriff Bullock shouted, leaping to his feet. "What's them serving or not serving in the military got to do with this?"

"I believe it has a lot to do with it, your honor, and I'll make it abundantly clear if I'm allowed to cross-examine this witness."

"Go ahead," the judge said.

"Answer the question,"
"No," the horse wrangler said softly.
"Could you speak up so the court can hear you?"
"NO!"
"*If* either of you *had* fought in the war, which side would you most likely have fought for?"
"The Union, of course!"
"In fact of the matter, you don't much like those that fought for the Confederacy, do you Mr. Sand?"
"Nope."
"What about your friends, Troy and Colby? They didn't like those that fought for the Confederacy either, did they?"
"Nope."
"In fact, while you and your two friends were drinking over in the saloon that day, the subject came up that Mr. Hawk here, was a captain in the Confederate Cavalry, didn't it?"
"Yeah, what if it did?"
"And your two friends decided they'd walk over and have a little fun with this *Johnny Reb,* didn't they?"
"I reckon."
"Why didn't you go with them?"
"I just didn't want to, that's all."
"No, you were *preoccupied* with a saloon girl named Rose, isn't that true?"
"What if I was, so what?"
"Mr. Sand, do you know what the word *perjury* means?"
"Of course I know what it means!"
"Your Honor, would you mind telling the witness the penalty for perjury?"

"Perjury is punishable by up to six months in jail," the judge said.

"*Six months!* That's a long, long time," Wade Henson said. "Mr. Sand, I want you to take your time before you answer my next question. Isn't it a fact that you only rushed across the street *after* you heard the gun shots and that you didn't see the gunfight at all?"

The horse wrangler hung his head and refused to answer.

"I can call Rose to the stand if I need to. She will testify that the two of you were together in the saloon when you heard the gun shots. Is that what you want?"

Benny Sand shook his lowered head.

"The court didn't hear your answer, Mr. Sand. Did you actually witness the gunfight at all, yes or no!"

Again, the witness shook his lowered head.

"No."

"I have no further questions for this witness," Wade Henson said.

"Sheriff, you may call your next witness," the judge said.

"I have no more witnesses," Sheriff Bullock said.

"Then the defense can call your first witness."

"I call Sheriff Sam Bullock," Mr. Henson said.

The sheriff jumped to his feet. His face flushed beet-red.

"But you can't call me as a witness for the defense, I'm the prosecutor!" the sheriff shouted loudly.

"Your Honor?" the attorney asked, turning toward the judge.

"I don't see why not," the judge ruled.

The court clerk swore the sheriff in and Sam Bullock sat down in the witness chair.

"Please state your name."

"Everybody knows my name. I'm Sam Bullock, sheriff of Monroe County."

"Did you have an occasion to witness a gunfight between Mr. Hawk, here, and Troy Head and Colby Middleton? Judge Little, would you remind the sheriff that he's under oath?"

"I think he knows that," the judge said.

"And please remind him that being the sheriff doesn't make immune to a perjury charge."

"I think he knows that, too."

"Very well, Sheriff Bullock, did either you or your deputy, Deuce Bailey, *actually witness* the gunfight?"

"Well, no, Troy Head and Colby Middleton were already dead when we arrived."

"Did you interview even *one* of the dozen or more witnesses who *actually* saw what happened? Isn't it a fact, Sheriff that several witnesses actually told you that Mr. Hawk acted in self defense and that Troy Head clearly drew first?"

"I don't remember."

"You don't remember. Well, I'm prepared to call a dozen witnesses who will testify under oath that they told you it was clearly self defense. You didn't bother interviewing even one witness, and yet you placed Mr. Hawk under arrest. Why would you do that, Sheriff?"

"I was just doing my duty."

"No, *Sheriff,* if you had done your *duty* my client would have never been arrested because you would have found out that he acted completely in self defense. Let's talk about my client getting beat and stomped half to death while he was in your custody. How do you suppose that happened, Sheriff?"

"My deputy left the jail unattended while he went to get something to eat. I suppose someone slipped in and beat up the prisoner while he was gone."

"You *suppose*! But wasn't it a policy *never* to leave the jail unattended when you had a prisoner?"

"It was."

"Then why would your deputy, who clearly knew what the policy was, leave the jail unattended and go have supper?"

"I don't know, you'll have to ask him."

"Well, as a matter of fact I *did* ask him. What do you suppose he said?"

"I have no idea. He's not the pick of the litter when it comes to smarts."

"Your former deputy told me that you told him to go on to supper, that you would cover for him until he got back. Did you tell him that, Sheriff?"

"I don't remember."

"*You don't remember!* You seem to have a very *convenient* lack of memory. The fact is you *arranged* that the jail be left unattended because you *knew* the so-called *night-riders* were going to come, didn't you Sheriff?"

"THAT'S A LIE!" the sheriff yelled.

"*Who* ordered you to leave the jail unattended? *Who* wanted Mr. Hawk beat up so bad maybe he would stop nosing around and asking questions?"

"I don't know what you're talking about!" the sheriff said, raising his voice and turning red-faced.

"I think you do. I think you know who gives the orders in this town. I think you know who sent the *night-riders* to hang John Hawk and burn his house and barns and to beat up Jubal Hawk! Who is it, Sheriff? Who pulls the strings in Monroe County?"

"MR. HENSON!" the judge said loudly. "You're badgering the witness. Stop it right now or I'll hold you in contempt!"

"I'm sorry, Your Honor. Since the sheriff hasn't presented one single witness that Mr. Hawk did not act in self-defense, I move that this case be dismissed."

"Do I hear any objections from the prosecution as to why I should not dismiss the charges against Mr. Hawk?"

The sheriff shook his head in silence.

"Case dismissed. Mr. Hawk, you are free to go."

Jubal shook his attorney's hand and hugged his younger brother. Lots of townfolk came around to shake Jubal's hand and congratulate him.

CHAPTER VI

Several weeks passed quickly. Ike and his helper were making swift progress on the new house. Jubal and Jason stayed close to their building site.

Determined to locate the horse herd the *night-riders* stole from the Hawk Ranch, Jubal began visiting the neighboring ranches.

The first one was the sprawling Box J Jessup Ranch that straddled McMinn and Monroe Counties near the town of Athens.

Shortly after riding onto the Jessup property he encountered a sign nailed to a tree warning trespassers they were on Jessup ranch property and would be shot.

Jubal heeled his buckskin and rode on.

He had ridden only a few miles before three riders boiled from a stand of pine trees and galloped toward him. Jubal reined up and waited.

All three riders carried Henry repeater rifles and looked more like fighting men than horse wranglers. They surrounded Jubal and reined to a stop. One of them rode a big black and white pinto.

"Mister, the land you're riding on is Box J land," one of the riders told him. He was a big man; Jubal guessed him to stand well over six feet. He had a Henry rifle propped against the swell of his saddle. He also wore a Remington handgun in a tied-down holster.

"Colonel Jessup don't take kindly to strangers. You best turn around and ride back the way you come from."

"I'm Jubal Hawk. I own the Diamond H Horse Ranch a few miles to the northwest. Some of our horses strayed. I'm looking for them."

"Well, you won't find them here. We don't take in stray horses. Like I said, you best turn that buckskin around and head back to your own place."

"I'd like to see your boss," Jubal persisted. "Since I'm already here, I'd like to be neighborly and meet him."

"The Colonel ain't the *neighborly* type."

"Let's let him decide that."

For a long moment the speaker sat his saddle, seemingly trying to decide what to do.

"Okay, it's your funeral, follow me," the man said, reining his pinto around and heeling it into a short lope. Jubal followed. The other two riders fell in behind Jubal.

They rode in silence for well over an hour. As they rode past several small herds of horses Jubal strained to see what brand they carried, but he was never close enough to tell if any of them wore the Diamond H brand.

Off in the distance atop a long, sloping hill, a sprawling cedar house dominated the surrounding area. It was impressive, much like the one they were building on the Hawk Ranch. A split-rail fence surrounded the house.

Several rows of barns with large corrals attached sat nearby. The corrals were full of horses.

"Wait here," the ranch foreman ordered as they reined up near a gate in the split rail fence.

He dismounted and headed up a tree-lined path leading to the house.

The door opened and the most beautiful young lady Jubal had ever seen stepped out onto the wide porch that ran along the entire front of the house.

Her long, blonde hair lifted in the soft breeze. She swiped it back in place with the back of her hand while staring at Jubal as he was staring at her. She wore a floor-length light blue dress with white lace around the neck and sleeves. She leaned casually against a cedar post and continued to stare at Jubal.

The big man went into the house for only a short moment before emerging and waving Jubal forward. He stepped to the ground, looped his reins around a hitching rail, and headed up the path toward the house.

The closer he got to the house, the more beautiful the lady looked. She was too young to be the Colonel's wife, so she must be his daughter, he decided. Her sparkling blue eyes were fixed upon him as he climbed the steps to the porch. She didn't move from her position against the post.

"Good morning," she said cheerfully. "We've never met. I'm Caroline Jessup."

"I'm Jubal Hawk. I have a horse ranch southeast of here. I came to see your father, but it's nice to meet you."

"Likewise," she said, her fixed gaze never leaving his eyes. "Perhaps we'll meet again."

A giant of a man with long, snow-white hair, a square-like face, and hard, pale eyes stepped through the front door onto the porch. He wore typical ranch clothes with a brown leather vest and western boots. He stuck out his big hand toward Jubal.

"I'm Colonel Jessup; I see you've already met my daughter. Come inside, Mr. Hawk, let's visit over a cup of coffee."

"Suits me fine," he said, not wanting to take his eyes off the daughter.

The Colonel led him inside the big house to a den. The big ranch foreman followed. Two leather couches faced one another in front of a floor-to-ceiling rock fireplace. A large, highly-polished desk sat in front of twin windows. Two overstuffed chairs sat in front of the desk. The Colonel motioned Jubal to one of the chairs while he took a leather upholstered chair behind the desk. Jubal noticed that the ranch foreman stood just inside the den, leaning against a wall.

"Actually, I'm glad you stopped by, Mr. Hawk, I've been wanting to talk with you."

"Oh, what about?"

"I've seen your ranch. It's ideally located in a beautiful valley with access to the river. I'm looking to expand my Box J ranch. I believe you have five hundred acres. I'd like to buy it."

"It's not for sale."

"Now, now, Mr. Hawk. Everything's for sale, it's just a matter of agreeing on the price."

"You're wrong. That property's been in the Hawk family for years. We would never sell it."

Jubal stood to his feet. His hand settled only a hair's breadth away from the pistol on his right hip. He shifted so he could see both the Colonel and the big foreman.

"A few months back, *night-riders* raided our ranch in the middle of the night. They hung my father, burned our house and barns, and stole over a hundred head of horses.

"The leader of the *night-riders* rode a black and white pinto, just like the one your man standing there rides. I'm gonna find out who those men were and I'm gonna kill them and the one that sent them. So I'm asking you straight out, did you send the *night-riders* to hang my father and burn our ranch?"

"I most certainly did not!" the Colonel said, jumping to his feet. "I don't have to resort to tactics like that to get what I want and I don't appreciate you coming to my home and accusing me of such a thing!"

"Then you won't mind if I look over the brands of some of your horses?"

"Yes, I do mind. I'm afraid you're no longer welcome here, Mr. Hawk. Good day to you, sir. My foreman will see you to our property line!"

"Hear me, Jessup, and hear me good. If I catch a *night-rider* wearing a hood on my property, I'll hang him from the nearest tree!"

"That's mighty big talk."

"I say what I mean and mean what I say."

The red-faced Colonel hurried from the room without another word, madder than an old setting hen.

The big foreman escorted Jubal from the house. The beautiful daughter no longer stood on the porch; Jubal went to his horse and swung into the saddle. Two of the first security men stayed with Jubal until they reached the edge of the Jessup Ranch.

I'll be seeing you again, boys, you can bank on it, Jubal thought, as he rode away.

* * *

Long days turned into weeks and weeks into months. Ike and his helper worked from sun-up to sun-down. The sprawling cedar home was something to see. According to Ike, it was the largest, most impressive home in eastern Tennessee.

"I've built lots of houses," the builder told Jubal, "but never anything like this one."

It was two stories, built in a square, with a flowered courtyard in the center. A natural spring fed a small fish pond and cistern for drinking water. The second floor had four bedrooms and a sitting room. A large den, dining room, kitchen, and the master bedroom were downstairs.

The floors were highly polished cedar and most of the furniture was made from cedar. A wide porch completely surrounded the house.

When the "Big House" as they called it, was finished, Jubal had Ike and his helper start two smaller cabins for Washington and a woman servant yet to be hired.

Jubal and Jason rode a circle of their property daily, watching closely for signs of any intruder. Twice lately, they had found tracks of somebody watching the house. Squashed cigarette butts in a thick stand of cedar trees told them somebody had spent long hours watching the progress of their new home.

"It's time we go and bring Mother and Mary Lou home," he told Jason. "Think you can handle that? I feel like I need to stay close for awhile."

"I sure can!" Jason said. "I'll take the wagon and leave at first light."

Jason left with the team and wagon as a new day peeked over the eastern horizon. His saddle horse was tied behind the wagon and his Henry rifle propped against the wagon seat.

"Keep your rifle handy and stay alert," Jubal told him.

Jubal stood and watched his younger brother until he was out of sight. He went to their makeshift corral, caught and saddled Buck, and rode toward the cedar thicket where they had spotted footprints. He ground hitched his horse in another nearby thicket, slipped his rifle from the saddle boot, and made his way to the spy's hiding place. He found a good-sized boulder with a good view of the intruder's hiding place and settled down for a long wait.

I might be wasting my time; he might not even come today. What could he be watching for? Who is it and what does he want? If I was guessing I'd say it's one of the Colonel's men, but why would he be spying on us?

Jubal thought about Jason. *Maybe I shouldn't have let him make that trip alone, but he's might near a grown man, he can take care of himself.*

The morning sun broke bright and clear. An hour passed—then two. Still no one showed up. Mid-morning came and went. He was just about to give up for the day when he heard a sound from the direction of the spy's hiding place. A horse snorted. A man appeared. He slipped along; his head swiveled back and forth cautiously. Finally, he squatted in his hiding place in a heavy stand of scrub cedar bushes.

Jubal carefully levered a shell into his rifle. He crawled forward on hands and knees, careful to avoid any dry twigs that would snap under his weight and alert the intruder.

When he was only thirty feet behind the man, he pushed up to his feet with his rifle trained on the intruder.

"Don't move!" he said loudly. "Drop that rifle or I'll kill you!"

The man snapped his head around, saw that he was covered, and dropped his rifle.

Jubal walked cautiously toward the man, careful to keep the intruder covered.

"Who are you? Why are you spying on us?"

"Just watching your house being built," the man said in a deep voice.

"You're one of the *night-riders* that hung my father and burned our house, ain't you?"

"Don't know nothing about no *night-riders*."

The man looked to be straddling forty, with a heavy beard.

"What's your name?" Jubal demanded.

"Swede Tully."

"Lets you and me walk over to your horse, Swede Tully."

"What for?"

"Just like to look your horse over, that's all."

Still keeping the intruder covered with his rifle, they walked over to the man's horse. It was a big strawberry roan. Jubal lifted the flap on the saddle bags tied behind the saddle and looked inside. Reaching a hand, he withdrew a toe-sack hood with holes cut to see through.

"Well, well," Jubal said, holding the hood up in front of the man. "Look what we have here. Just like the ones the *night-riders* wear. I'm gonna ask you a question just once. If you lie to me I'll kill you. Do you understand?"

The frightened man nodded understanding.

"Who do you work for?"

"I can't tell you that, they'd kill me!"

"I'm gonna kill you if you don't. It's your choice."

The man hesitated for a moment. Jubal lashed out with the butt of his Henry. The blow struck the man on his right ear, knocking him to the ground.

For a long minute the man studied on his situation. While he did, Jubal whistled for his horse. It took only a minute until Buck trotted up to him. Jubal untied a lariat from his saddle and began fashioning a hangman's noose. The man watched in silence. Great drops of sweat suddenly appeared on his forehead. He licked dry lips and shifted from one foot to the other.

"Time's up," Jubal said, dropping the noose over the man's head and sliding the knot tight around his neck. Jubal cut a short rope from the loose end of the lariat and tied the man's hands behind his back.

"Get up in the saddle," Jubal ordered.

"What are you gonna do?" the frightened man asked frantically.

"I'm gonna hang you," Jubal told him.

"But . . . but . . . you can't do that! I ain't done nothing!"

"I asked you a question. I ain't heard the answer."

The man had trouble mounting. Jubal helped him before mounting his own horse. He led the man several miles toward Sweetwater to a giant sycamore tree only a few feet from the edge of the main road leading to town.

He reined up and tossed the loose end of the rope over a sturdy limb. He stretched the rope tight and tied it off to the trunk of the tree.

"You can't do this! It ain't right! I didn't do nothing!"

"Last chance," he told the frightened man.

"Please don't kill me, mister, please. I'll tell you anything you want to know, but please don't hang me!"

"Who do you work for?"

"I . . . I work for . . . Colonel Jessup."

"Were you there when they hung my father and burned our home?"

The man nodded.

"But I didn't do it! Vance is the one that hung your pa, Vance Slater."

"Who else was there?"

"Gus Worley, Max Carlyle, Joe Swain, and Blackie Cain."

"Where are the horses you fellows stole from us?"

"We hid 'em in a little valley on the backside of the Colonel's ranch. Coker Creek runs through the valley."

"You done good," Jubal said, jamming the toe-sack hood over the man's head. "Now you can die with a clear conscious."

He swatted the man's horse. The *night-rider* screamed. The animal leaped forward, dragging the rider from his saddle. Jubal watched as the man pawed the air with his feet, searching for footing, but finding only empty air as he swung back and forth. A gurgled scream escaped the condemned man's lips and then—nothing. Jubal left him hanging as a warning sign—and rode away.

"That's one," he said aloud, as he rode away.

CHAPTER VII

The "Big House" was finished and ready for the Hawk family to move in. Ike had furnished each room with hand-polished cedar furniture.

The following morning Jason arrived with Mrs. Hawk and Mary Lou. Both were overwhelmed with their new home. Jubal's mother stood alone by the rocking chair that would have been her husband's and shed sad tears.

Ike and his helper had the servant quarters almost finished and was about to start on the barns.

Two days after their mother's return, Jubal and Jason saddled up and headed out to find their stolen horse herd. Jubal hadn't mentioned anything about the Jessup rider and that he had hung the man.

"How do you know where to look?" Jason asked as they rode.

"I just got me a gut-wrenchin' hunch," Jubal told him. They headed due south along the foothills of the Appalachian Mountain Range. Knowing there would be Box J riders assigned to watch over the herd, Jubal and Jason kept to the timber as much as possible.

It was mid-afternoon when they came upon a freshwater creek Jubal figured had to be Coker Creek. It rushed down from the high country and wound through an opening between two steep mountains into a small, but beautiful little valley. A thin tendril of smoke trailed lazily upward from a small log cabin nestled among a cluster of tall, stately pine trees at the far end of the valley.

A large herd of horses grazed peacefully on hock-high grass. Jubal and Jason circled the herd, working their way close enough to check the brands—sure enough—the horses wore their Diamond H brand.

A magnificent coal-black stallion stood apart from the herd. He tossed his head and pawed the ground, moving about nervously at the intruders who dared venture near his herd.

"That's *King,* our stud," Jubal said. "No doubt about it, it's been a long time, but I'd recognize him anywhere."

Now that they knew for sure the horses belonged to them, the problem would be how to get them out of the valley and back to the Hawk Ranch without a run-in with Colonel Jessup's riders.

Keeping to the bushes, they worked their way closer to the cabin. A small corral held only two saddled horses which eased Jubal's mind that only two riders guarded the stolen herd. Jubal and Jason tied their horses in a thicket and, taking their rifles, crept closer.

"Stay here and cover me," Jubal told Jason. "I'm gonna try to work my way closer."

Bending low, Jubal moved from one clump of low-lying bushes to another. He cautiously approached from a blind side of the cabin and pressed his back against the wall of the cabin. He levered a shell into his rifle and approached the only door in the log structure.

Lifting a booted foot, he kicked the door in and quickly followed the door inward.

Two men sat at a makeshift table sipping coffee. They leaped to their feet as Jubal rushed into the room. One fellow jerked a pistol from its holster. Jubal shot the man in the chest. The man slammed backward onto the dirt floor and didn't move. The second fellow was young, most likely younger that Jason. He quickly raised his hands.

"Are you two the only ones here?" Jubal asked, stepping forward and removing the young man's gun.

He stared at Jubal and nodded his head. Jubal scanned the small, one room cabin. Only two bedrolls were visible on makeshift cots; it seemed the young man was telling the truth.

"What's your name?" Jubal demanded.

"Billy Bob Wheeler."

"What about your partner? What was his name?"

"Shorty James," the man answered. Neither of them matched the names given him as being part of the *night-riders* that raided the Hawk Ranch.

Jubal went to the door and called out to Jason.

"Come on in, Jason, and bring our horses."

When Jason arrived leading their two horses, Jubal cut a small rope from a lariat and tied the Jessup rider's hands behind his back.

"What are you gonna do with me?" the frightened young man asked.

"Where you from, Billy?"

"My folks live the other side of the mountains in North Carolina."

"Don't know about North Carolina, but in Tennessee, we hang horse thieves. We find you guarding a herd of horses stolen from our ranch. We've got every right to hang you from the nearest tree."

"Yes, sir," the frightened young man answered softly.

"What would you do if our places were reversed?" Jubal asked.

The young fellow just shook his lowered head slowly.

"How far you figure it is to your folks' place?"

"Forty, maybe fifty miles."

"I'm gonna cut you some slack this time, Billy, but if I ever see you again I'll kill you, no questions asked! Do you understand me?"

The young fellow nodded his head.

"Go get on your horse and head for home. Like I said, if I see you again I'll shoot you on sight. Now get out of here before I change my mind."

Jubal and Jason rounded up the herd of horses and pointed them toward home.

They followed the Little Tennessee River and moved the herd of horses slowly. It was near sundown when, as they topped a wooded hill and headed down the other side, Jubal spotted a familiar scene he remembered from his growing-up years. It was a waterfall where the river broke over a rock shelf and tumbled forty feet to form a wide pool of crystal-clear water. He remembered many times spending hot afternoons in the cool, clear water. The banks on both sides were moss-covered.

"What a beautiful place," Jason exclaimed. "I never knew this was here."

"I used to come here when I was your age and had something on my mind to work out," Jubal told him. "I called it my *thinking place*."

"Is this on our land?" Jason asked.

"No, but it's so isolated I doubt very few even know about it."

"It sure is a pretty place," Jason said.

"We need to get these horses moving and get them back to our ranch," Jubal said. "It'll be dark soon."

"I'm glad you let that boy go," Jason said, as they rode side by side behind the horse herd. "He looked even younger than me."

"I don't think he was really a bad boy, he just got mixed up with the wrong bunch. That's easy to do when you're young."

"Do you think those *night-riders* will bother us again?"

"Mor'n apt. We'll just have to stay on our toes and keep our eyes open."

"I'm shore glad you're home, Jubal," Jason told him.

"Me too," Jubal said.

It was already dark when they arrived at the ranch. King, their magnificent coal-black stallion led his horse herd into the largest corral near the main barn. Mrs. Hawk and the others hurried outside to watch.

King was a full seventeen hands high and weighed north of sixteen hundred pounds. When the young colt was born, John Hawk took one look and said, "This colt is going to be the king of the Hawk Ranch, so his name should be *King*."

Over the years, King had sired many champion Tennessee Walker horses and made the Hawk Ranch a small fortune.

The big stallion tossed his head, reared up on his hind legs, and pawed the air, as if he was glad to have his herd of prime mares back where they belonged.

Their trained Tennessee Walker horses were famous far and wide and had provided an excellent living for the Hawk family for years. Both Jubal and Jason had grown up perfecting the art of training the breed of walking horses under the watchful eye of their father. John Hawk was recognized all over the country as a top horse trainer.

Jubal knew and accepted that it was his and his brother's duty to carry his father's legacy forward.

The Hawk family gathered around the large dining table that was crowded with bowls of steaming food. The meal was mixed with laughter and happy conversation. When the meal was over, Jubal tapped his glass with the blade of a knife for attention. He rose and let his slow gaze move over each member of the family. Emotion gave birth to a large lump that crawled up his throat and lodged there. He cleared his throat.

"I just want to tell you how very proud I am to be back home. I'm sorry I wasn't here to help protect Pa and our home. I'll never forgive myself for that and promise you I won't allow anything like that to ever happen again.

"I'm going to hunt down those that are responsible and see they pay for it. I won't rest until every last one of them is brought to justice. Now, would you join me in lifting our glasses in a toast to the man that built this ranch, our father, John Hawk?"

CHAPTER VIII

Less than a week after Jubal hung the *night-rider,* Sheriff Sam Bullock and his new deputy reined up in front of the Hawk Ranch house. The deputy Jubal remembered from the trial had a sawed-off double-barrel shotgun propped upright against his leg.

"Hello, the house!" the sheriff called out loudly.

Jubal heard him and stepped to the front door with his Henry rifle in the crook of his arm. Jason also heard the call and appeared in the doorway of a nearby barn, also armed with his rifle.

"We found a dead man with a toe-sack hood hanging from a tree just outside town a few days ago," the sheriff said. "Don't reckon you'd know anything about it?"

"Why would I know anything about it?" Jubal asked, leaning a shoulder against a porch post.

"Could be because I heard you threatened to hang anybody that trespassed on your property."

"Your boss, Colonel Jessup, tell you that?"

"Don't matter none where I heard it. I come to warn you, Hawk, you start taking the law into your own hands and you'll answer to me."

"Is that supposed to scare me, Sheriff?"

"You been warned!" the sheriff said loudly, roughly reining his mount around. The deputy followed his boss as they short-loped away.

"What was he talking about?" Jason asked, walking up while watching the two riders as they rode away.

"He said they found a man near town that had been hung. Sounded like he thought we had something to do with it."

"I don't like that man," Jason said.

"You won't get any argument outta me on that score," Jubal agreed.

The house and barns were finished. Jubal paid his carpenter and the helper for a fine job and promised to use them again should he need any more building done.

Their horse herd had settled in. Jubal, Jason, and Wash set about the chore of selecting the prime breeding mares and, when they were ready for breeding, putting them in with King, their stud.

Later in their pregnancy, they would be separated from the herd, stalled, groomed, and fed a special diet to insure proper development of the foal. It required long and tedious hours to care for a herd as large as theirs.

Mrs. Hawk and Mary Lou seemed happy in their new home. The entire Hawk family continued their tradition of having supper together each evening. They used that important time to discuss family matters and decisions that affected the entire family.

Two more of their former slaves, Lilly Armstrong and her daughter Myra, returned after failing to find work elsewhere. Jubal hired the mother and grown daughter to serve as their cook and housekeeper. They moved into the brand new cabin built just for that purpose.

Jubal continued to make daily rides around the far reaches of their ranch checking for trespassers. On one such ride he spotted a rider on a snow-white horse on a distant hillside. The rider was too far away to identify, so he slipped his rifle from the saddle boot and rode closer.

When he closed the distance he discovered the rider was a woman—it was the beautiful daughter of Colonel Jessup that he had met earlier—Caroline Jessup. He reined up nearby and touched thumb and finger to the brim of his hat.

"Morning, ma'am."

"Good morning. Mr. Hawk, isn't it? It's such an absolutely perfect day I thought I would go for a ride."

Jubal flicked a glance upward to the blue sky and bright, warm sun.

"It is a beautiful day for a ride. It's good to see you again. To be perfectly honest, I was hoping I might run into you again."

"Oh?"

"We didn't have an opportunity to visit when we met earlier."

"No, we didn't. My father seemed rather upset after you left."

"I'm afraid we don't see eye to eye on some things."

"He hasn't been the same since my mother died."

"I'm sorry for your loss. How long has she been gone?"

"It's been two years now. I was away at school when it happened."

"I see. I'm surprised he would let you go riding alone without an escort."

"Why would I need an escort?"

"There's been a lot of bad things going on around here lately. It might not be safe for a lady riding alone."

"What kind of *bad things*?"

"They found a man that had been hanged over near Sweetwater just a few days ago. Not long ago a bunch of *night-riders* with toe-sack hoods over their faces burned our house and barns, hung my father, and stole our herd of horses."

Jubal watched her face closely to see if she already knew about the raid. Shock showed clearly on her face. Clearly she had not heard of the tragic events.

"Oh," she exclaimed. "I'm sorry. That must have been a terrible time for your family."

"Yes, ma'am, it was."

"I'd love to meet your wife sometime," she said, searching his eyes with hers.

"I'm not married. I just returned from the war. I wasn't here when they hung my father."

"Oh, I see. And to come home to find what happened to your father and your home destroyed, how awful!"

"Yes, ma'am, it was. Will you feel comfortable riding with me? I'd like to show you something."

"Of course."

They rode side by side and visited until they came upon the waterfall that Jubal used to visit as a youngster. They reined up on the mossy bank of the river.

"What a beautiful place!" she exclaimed, wide-eyed.

Jubal marveled at her lake-blue eyes. When she smiled one edge of her lips lifted in a way that looked like she was pouting. She noticed him staring at her.

"What's wrong?" she asked, wrinkling her eye brows with a questioning look.

"Nothing . . . nothing at all, I was just admiring your smile. It's so unusual."

She laughed out loud.

"What's wrong with my smile?"

"Nothing, it's just . . . *unusual*," he quickly apologized. "It's sort of a *mischievous pouting* smile. It's beautiful."

"Thank you, kind sir," she said, looking quickly away with an embarrassed look.

He dismounted and reached a hand to help her down. She accepted his hand and swung to the ground. They ground-hitched their horses and strolled slowly to a large boulder near the edge of the river.

"How did you know about this place?" she asked. "Have you been here before?"

"I used to come here and swim when I was growing up," he explained.

She leaned over and touched a hand in the water and jerked it back quickly.

"It's so cold! How did you stand swimming in it?"

"You get used to it after a few minutes."

"I'm not sure I could, it gives me chill bumps just to touch it with my hand. This is such a beautiful place. Would you mind if I came here again sometime?"

"This isn't on my land. I'm not sure who it belongs to, but I'm sure whoever it is, they wouldn't mind. There's a shallow opening behind the waterfall, kinda like a cave. Sometimes I used to sit in there and listen to the crashing water and pretend it was my secret place and that no one knew about it except me."

"Did you come here alone?"

"Yes, I used to years ago. This is only the second time I've been here since I returned from the war."

"How long were you gone?"

"Almost five years."

"Was it terrible?"

"Yes, ma'am, lots of men lost their lives."

"I've never understood why men go to war. It's never made sense to me."

"I thought I knew what we were fighting for when I went, but looking back on it now, I'm not so sure."

"Which side did you fight for?" she asked.

"I was a captain in the Confederate cavalry."

"My father supported the Union."

"Yes, ma'am, I know. There's still a lot of bitterness in these parts about the war."

"But the war is over. There's no reason we can't be friends is there?"

"Not as far as I'm concerned. But I'm not sure your father would feel the same way."

"Why would he object if we were friends?"

"I'm afraid he don't like me very much."

"Maybe that's because he doesn't know you."

"Maybe."

"Maybe we'll run into each other again sometime," she said, locking her eyes on his for a brief moment. "I go riding most every day."

"I'd like that," he said.

"But right now, I need to go. My father will be worried. I have really enjoyed our visit."

"Me too," he said, reaching a hand to help her up from the rock. Their hands touched for only a fleeting moment, but the thrill of that touch was like a lightning bolt that raced all the way to his heart.

They walked slowly to her white horse and he helped her mount, holding her hand a little longer than necessary, but she didn't seem to object.

She lifted the reins and paused for a long moment. Her eyes found his and lingered there. No words were spoken, but something in the look told him that she was sharing the same feelings he was. She suddenly reined her mount around and galloped away.

He watched her until she disappeared from sight. He slowly returned to the rock and sat for a long time, revisiting the memory of what just happened. He knew without a doubt his life would never be the same after meeting her.

CHAPTER IX

After the accidental meeting with Caroline Jessup, Jubal thought of her constantly. Whether working around the ranch, riding, or just relaxing, thoughts of her occupied his mind. He went for a long ride each day, hoping to run into her again.

Three days after their meeting, he was sitting in the porch swing on the front porch after supper with a cup of coffee. He glanced up at the moon and determined it was past midnight. Everyone else had long since gone to bed.

Suddenly he heard King whinny. The stallion was clearly upset about something. He set his coffee down and hurried to the barn to see what had disturbed their big stallion.

Light from a three-quarter moon outlined the silhouette of two men outside King's stall.

"Don't move!" Jubal shouted, snatching his Colt from its holster.

He hurried closer to the intruders, careful to keep them covered. The men stood motionless with their hands in the air.

A movement behind him caused Jubal to glance around quickly—it was Wash.

"What is it Master Hawk, sir?" the black man asked anxiously.

"We've got a couple of visitors," Jubal told him. "Get a lantern from the wall beside the door and light it."

Wash did as Jubal asked and brought the lantern closer. Toe-sack hoods covered the men's faces.

"Decided to pay us another visit, eh?" Jubal said. "What was it this time, gonna burn the barn again?"

Neither of the men said anything. Jubal noticed something in one of the men's hands—it was a small can with a lid on it. He took it from the man and looked closer—the label read *Sodium Cyanide* and had a picture of a skull and crossbones on it—he had seen it before in the war—it was poison—one of the most lethal poisons known to man.

"Poison!" Jubal said through clenched teeth and a set jaw. "You were about to poison our stud! Get some rope and tie their hands," he told Wash.

After the men were securely tied with their hands behind their backs, Jubal told Wash to saddle his buckskin and find the two men's horses. Once Wash brought their horses in from a nearby grove of trees and had saddled Jubal's buckskin, they helped the two intruders into their saddles.

"Go back to bed," Jubal told his colored friend. "Don't say anything to the others about this."

Jubal swung into his saddle and gathered the reins to the *night-rider's* horses. As he rode from the barn he took two lariats from wall pegs beside the door.

He judged it to be near daylight when he reined up just outside Sweetwater. He sat his saddle for a few minutes and listened to the sounds of the night. Leading the two *night-riders'* horses underneath the large sycamore tree where he had hanged the other *night-rider*, he threw the two ropes from his barn over a sturdy limb.

"You ain't gonna hang us!" one of the men protested. "We ain't done nothing!"

"Shut your mouth," the second man told his partner. "I told you what we was gonna do was wrong! I don't cotton to poisoning a horse!"

"What's your name, mister?" Jubal asked.

"I'm Joe Swain."

"What's your partner's name?"

"Max Carlyle."

"Both of you were in the bunch that burned our home and hung my father, weren't you?"

"I don't know what you're talking about," the man lied, but Jubal remembered their names from the first *night-rider* he hung.

He made a loop in the end of a lariat and dropped it over the hooded head of the speaker.

"Please, mister, we didn't mean you no harm! Please don't hang us!"

His words fell on deaf ears as Jubal dropped the second loop over the man's head and cinched it tight. Without another word, Jubal swatted the backside of the two horses.

One of the men's pleas were choked off into a gurgling scream as both men were dragged from their saddles. They thrashed the air with their booted feet as they swung back and forth. In short minutes the only sound that disturbed the night was the faint sound of the two ropes as they rubbed against the limb under the weight of the two dead bodies.

Jubal reined his buckskin toward town and rode to the outskirts before entering Sweetwater Creek. As dawn broke he rode upstream for a mile or more before exiting on a rock shelf. Anyone trying to track him would have a difficult time.

The sun was noon-high when the posse charged into the yard in front of the Hawk home. A cloud of dust slowly settled around the riders as Jubal and Jason stepped from the house onto the front porch with rifles in their hands.

Jubal let his gaze crawl slowly over the men. Sheriff Bullock and his deputy sat their horses at the head of the pack. Beside the sheriff, Colonel Jessup sat his golden palomino. He wore a holster holding a pearl-handled Colt. Beside him, Vance Slater sat atop his big black and white pinto. Several other riders that Jubal figured rode for Jessup held rifles propped upright against their legs. Jubal estimated the posse contained a dozen men—far too many for a fight.

"I warned you not to meddle in my business!" Sheriff Bullock said loudly. "You're under arrest, Hawk!"

"Arrest?" Jubal said. "What for?"

"We found two of the Colonel's men hanging from a tree outside town this morning."

"What's that got to do with me?"

"It's clear to me you done it, that's what!"

"I was right here all night," Jubal told him. "I've got a half-dozen witnesses that will swear to it."

"You have no idea who you are messing with," Colonel Jessup spoke up and said.

"I could say the same to you, *Jessup,*" Jubal said, locking his hard gaze on the Colonel's pale eyes.

"Say the word, Colonel," Vance Slade said, "and we'll get this over and done with right here—right now." His dark eyes fixed upon Jubal.

"Anytime, Slade, anytime," Jubal said, accepting the clear challenge.

"No," the Colonel said. "We'll let the law handle it. You *are* going to handle it, aren't you Sheriff?"

"Yes, sir," Bullock said quickly, withdrawing his pistol and dismounting. He climbed the steps to the porch and stood in front of Jubal with a pistol in one hand and handcuffs in the other.

"Hold out your hands!" he ordered.

"Jason, go get my lawyer," Jubal told his brother as he held out his hands to the sheriff.

As the sheriff led Jubal away, Jason ran to the barn to saddle his horse for the ride to Lenoir City.

They lifted Jubal onto the deputy's horse forcing the man to ride double with one of Jessup's men. Upon reaching Sweetwater they roughly pulled Jubal from the saddle and shoved him before them into the familiar jail cell.

Once the door was locked, Colonel Jessup walked up to the cell and looked at Jubal through the bars with a snarling stare.

"You are not going to hang my men and get away with it. I will see to it."

Jubal glanced quickly around to insure no one else could hear his words.

"You sent two of your men to poison our stallion. What kind of man would *poison a horse?* They paid for what they were about to do. I'll hang every man you send to do your dirty work—then I'm coming after you! That's a promise!"

"We'll see how tough you are—we'll see!"

Jessup's face turned beet red. He sputtered something incoherent before abruptly turning on his heels and stalking away.

By late afternoon Wade Henson arrived. Jubal heard the loud voices even before the heavy door opened and the attorney entered the jail area.

"Let's go," the attorney told Jubal. "Your bail has been posted and you're free to go until the trial. Actually, I seriously doubt there will even be a trial. By their own admission they have absolutely no evidence that you're guilty of anything."

Sheriff Bullock didn't say a word as he handed Jubal the Colt and holster he had taken from him when the arrest was made.

"Jake Foley was with the posse that discovered the men that were hanged," the attorney told Jubal. "He said both of them were obviously part of the group they're calling the *night-riders*. He said both had toe-sack hoods over their heads."

"That's the bunch that hung my father and burned us out," Jubal said.

"Mr. Foley said both of them worked for Colonel Jessup, owner of the Box J Ranch."

"That don't surprise me," Jubal told him. "Jessup tried to buy our ranch. I told him no. Reckon he'll try to get it some other way."

"That makes three of the *night-riders* to end up swinging from the same tree. *Somebody* sure don't like them."

"*Nobody* likes them, but *somebody's* giving the orders," Jubal told the attorney. "Looks to me like *Colonel* Jessup is the prime suspect since all of them worked for him."

"All the evidence points that way. Well, I better be getting back to Lenoir City. Let me know if I can be of more help."

"I will," Jubal assured him. "Thanks."

Jason was waiting outside the sheriff's office with Jubal's horse. He mounted and they headed back to the ranch as darkness settled over the land.

Other than his daily circuit around the ranch property, Jubal stayed close for the next several days. There was always more work than there was daylight. Jubal, Jason, and Wash all worked from sun-up until well after sun-down.

It had been a long week. On Sunday afternoon Jubal decided to take a ride around the ranch. As he emerged from a thick stand of pine trees along a hillside, he spotted Caroline Jessup on her snow-white mare off in a distant valley. An instant feeling of excitement raced through him. In the back of his mind he had secretly hoped he might run into her again, but in reality he knew the chances were slim.

He reined up and waited for her to ride nearer. She spotted him and lifted an arm in greeting. Jubal heeled his big buckskin toward her, secretly thrilled at the accidental meeting.

Caroline Jessup's heart skipped a beat when she spotted the big buckskin off in the distance. Her face flushed warm with anticipation. Ever since their first accidental meeting she had thought of little else except Jubal Hawk.

She had met several young men during her two years at the private school for ladies in Philadelphia, but none of them aroused any interest whatsoever; Jubal Hawk was quite another matter.

He was tall and extremely handsome with his long, shoulder length, corn silk hair and sky-blue eyes that seemed to look right into her very soul. Just the brief moments when their eyes met sent chill-bumps racing across her skin.

She dampened her lips with a flick of her tongue as they drew closer. She lifted the corner of her lips in the mischievous *pouting* smile, as he had described it at their first meeting. To her, there was nothing unusual about her smile, but if he thought so that was enough for her.

She had taken great care dressing for her ride today hoping she might *accidently* run into him again. She wore black riding pants and boots; she refused to use the *lady-like* sidesaddles most ladies of her day used. She was raised on a horse ranch and had used western-style saddles since she was a little girl. In fact, she could ride and rope as well as any man on the ranch.

Her white silk blouse buttoned down the front and was tucked into her riding pants at the waist. A long, black ribbon held her long, blonde hair pulled back and hanging down her back.

"Out for a Sunday afternoon ride?" he greeted.

"Yes. It's such a lovely day for a ride, isn't it?"

"Yes, ma'am. Were you headed for the waterfall?" he asked.

"Yes, it's such a beautiful place."

"Mind if we ride together?"

"Not at all, I would enjoy your company. Besides, you could protect me in the event some of those *hooded* men came along," she said jokingly.

"I'm somewhat surprised your father would allow you to ride out here alone. Are you sure he don't send one of his men to watch over you?" he asked, flicking a searching look at the distant tree line.

"I don't think so; at least I haven't seen anyone except you."

"Maybe not," Jubal said, reining his buckskin to a slow walk beside the white mare.

They rode slowly, talking mostly about her white mare. They soon arrived at the river below the waterfall.

He dismounted and then reached a hand to help her to the ground. She offered her hand to him—he took it. It was soft as down feathers. As she reached the ground their hands remained together for the briefest moment.

Was he imagining it or did she squeeze his hand slightly before releasing it? Probably just his imagination, he thought.

His question about the possibility that her father might send one of his men to watch over her from a distance disturbed her.

Would he do that? If so, whoever he sent would surely report to her father about her meeting with Jubal. I've done nothing wrong, but I know Father doesn't like Jubal, although I have no idea why.

She quickly dismissed the thought from her mind. Jubal had been a perfect gentleman. She glanced down to see his offered hand to assist her in dismounting—she took it and stepped lightly to the ground. For a fleeting moment their hands remained together. She felt her face flush crimson and felt a tingle all the way down to her toes. Without even thinking, she felt her fingers tighten in a slight squeeze.

Their eyes met—and held for a moment. She felt a blush warm her face before breaking eye contact and looking toward the ground.

Jubal felt a knot race upward and lodge in his throat. He swallowed—and then swallowed again. Slowly, they walked casually to the water's edge. Jubal bent to pick up a small, flat rock and skipped it across the top of the water.

"Did you make a wish?" she asked.

"A *wish*?" Jubal replied.

"Yes, if you make a wish before the rock sinks legend says it will come true."

Jubal bent to pick up another rock and handed it to Caroline.

"Here, you try it."

She drew back an arm and skipped the rock expertly across the water.

"Well?" he asked. "What did you wish?"

"You're not supposed to tell, silly!"

"Then how will I know if your wish comes true?"

She was silent for a long moment.

"You'll know," she told him as her eyes lifted and made contact with his.

Jubal smiled and nodded acceptance of her answer, but wondered what she had meant by her words.

CHAPTER X

It was the deepest part of the night when they came. Jubal was awakened by the urgent ringing of one of the iron triangle alarms that he had placed in three locations: on the front porch of the main house, in front of Wash's cabin, and in the opening of the barn door.

He hastily climbed from bed and pulled on his britches before racing from his bedroom. As he reached the front door he grabbed his Henry rifle that always hung above the door facing. Levering a shell into the chamber, he jerked open the front door.

The ringing was coming from Wash's cabin. A single rifle shot suddenly silenced the ringing. Jubal saw the muzzle blast from the darkness near the barn. Slamming his rifle to his shoulder he triggered a quick shot at the location and was rewarded by a muffled scream from the shooter.

Jubal spotted a fire in the runway of the nearby barn at the same time he heard running bare feet behind him.

"What is it, Jubal?" Jason shouted as he rushed from the front door with a rifle in his hand.

"Raiders!" Jubal shouted as both of them raced barefooted toward the barn. "I think they got Wash! Go check on him and I'll take care of the fire! Be careful! I don't know how many there are!"

Another rifle shot rang out from the runway of the barn. It singed the air only inches from Jubal's ear. He snapped off a cover shot from waist level and ran in a zigzag pattern as fast as his bare feet could carry him. Jason veered off to the right toward Wash's cabin as Jubal reached the barn and plastered his back against the outside wall.

He immediately belly-flopped to the ground and snapped a look around the edge of the double-door opening. Light from the burning straw piled against the back wall of the barn illuminated the runway as bright as day and clearly outlined a hooded *night-rider* with a rifle pointed at the opening where Jubal lay.

Frantic whinnies and thrashing of hooves from a dozen prime mares pierced the night. They were trapped in their stalls along the runway of the barn. Popping sounds from the fresh pine of the barn wall told Jubal the back wall of the barn had caught. Hungry flames were licking their way upward on the wall.

If we don't get that fire out real quick we'll lose the barn and all our mares too, his mind screamed at him. He quickly levered another shell into his Henry, took a deep breath, and with reckless abandon threw his body into a flat roll directly into the opening of the wide double-door of the runway.

His action drew a quick shot from the *night-rider*. The slug plowed a furrow in the ground no more than an inch from Jubal's left shoulder. He returned fire from his prone position. Jubal's shot didn't miss.

The hooded *night-rider* suddenly arched backward and dropped his rifle. A spray of crimson exploded from the man's back. He staggered a half-step before his legs buckled and he went down.

Jubal leapt to his feet and grabbed a wooden bucket sitting beside a barrel full of water they kept near the entrance of the runway. He raced toward the fire, splashed the water on it, and returned again and again until the flames were reduced to thin whiffs of smoke.

The sound of galloping horses from somewhere behind the barn told him at least two or more of the attackers were getting away. He knew they would already be swallowed up by the darkness and that he had no chance of following whoever it was until daylight.

As soon as the fire was extinguished, Jubal raced from the barn toward Wash's cabin. A lamp from inside the cabin cast an elongated square on the ground outside the single window.

Jubal shoved the door open.

Lilly Armstrong and her daughter, Myra, Jubal's mother and Mary Lou were all crowded around a bunk near a potbellied stove—on the bunk lay Jubal's friend, Washington Jefferson, their longtime faithful servant. Jason stood near the door with his rifle.

Jubal's mother twisted a look at him as he entered. The sad look on her face answered his question without it being asked. She slowly shook her head—Wash was gone.

Jubal turned toward the door.

"Leave everything as it is," he said. "Don't touch anything. I'll be back."

He hurried to the house, dressed, and buckled his Colt sidearm around his waist. He went to the barn and saddled Buck, his big buckskin. He slammed his Henry rifle in the saddle boot and toed a stirrup. He heeled the buckskin into a short lope.

The eastern sky was painted with a rosy-orange color as he rode into Sweetwater. He reined up in front of Doctor Wilson's combination office and living quarters and rapped on the door until the doctor opened the door.

"There's been another raid on our ranch," Jubal said. "Get dressed and meet me in front of Marvin Stringfellow's house."

"I'll be right there," the doctor said.

Jubal then rode to a large, white, two-story house near the edge of town. He tied his buckskin to the hitching rail out front and stepped through the gate in the white picket fence that surrounded the big house. He climbed the steps to the front porch and knocked on the door.

It took a few minutes, but the banker finally opened the front door.

"I'm sorry to wake you this time of morning, but I need your help," Jubal told him.

"What's wrong, Jubal?"

"The *night-riders* raided our ranch again early this morning. They killed one of my men and tried to burn our barn. I'm gonna try to get the sheriff to do something about it, but I'm asking you and Doctor Wilson to come along as witnesses. Would you do that for us?"

"Of course," the banker said without hesitation. "Come inside and give me a few minutes to get dressed."

Jubal removed his hat and stepped into the living room. He sat down in a large, upholstered chair and circled his hat brim between thumb and finger until the banker returned.

When they stepped outside, Doctor Wilson was waiting in his black buggy. Together, the three of them went to the sheriff's office. Light from a lamp inside the office showed through the single window near the front door. Jubal pushed the door open.

Sheriff Bullock was dressed and pouring himself a cup of coffee from a blackened coffee pot when Jubal entered.

"What you want?" the lawman asked gruffly.

"*Night-riders* raided our ranch again early this morning. They killed one of my people and tried to burn our barn."

"How you know it was the *night-riders*?" Bullock questioned.

"Because I killed two of them, that's how. They're still wearing their toe-sack hoods."

"I'll ride out after awhile and look into it," the lawman said, blowing on his hot coffee and slouching into his desk chair.

"That ain't good enough," Jubal said between clenched teeth and palming his Colt. "You're coming with me *now*!"

"Now you just hold on! I ain't going *nowhere* at the point of a gun! I could arrest you for threatening a law enforcement officer!"

"You're *coming* if I have to hog-tie you and drag you! Now *move* before I forget you're a *law enforcement officer*! Marvin Stringfellow and Doc Wilson are coming along to serve as witnesses just so the story don't get bent out of shape later on."

"Oh," the lawman muttered as Jubal shoved him out the door and he saw the two city councilmen.

Bullock wasn't happy about it, but he cinched his saddle and reluctantly climbed up. The sun was peeking over the horizon as the little procession made their way out of town. Jubal, the banker, and Doctor Wilson carried on a conversation during the trip with them asking details about the raid, but the sheriff rode in silence.

As Jubal had instructed, everything had been left exactly as it was following the attack. The two dead *night-riders* still lay where they had fallen. Their hoods were still in place over their heads.

Jubal and the two city councilmen stood around the body as Sheriff Bullock removed the hood from the first attacker's head.

"I know that fellow," Doctor Wilson exclaimed. "His name is Blackie Cain. He works for Colonel Jessup on the Box J Ranch. He had a bad cut on his leg a couple of months back and I sewed it up."

Sheriff Bullock said nothing. He just threw the hood down beside the body and made his way to the other dead man and jerked his hood off.

"Anybody know this one?" the sheriff asked.

Doctor Wilson and Marvin Stringfellow both shook their heads.

"Never seen that one before," they both agreed.

Jubal showed them the end of the barn that was burned and would have to be replaced.

"You said one of your people was killed?" the sheriff questioned.

"Yes, come with me."

They all made their way to the small cabin and went inside. The black, former slave lay on the bunk. Someone had covered him with a blanket.

"His name is Washington Jefferson," Jubal told them. "He's worked for our family for many years."

Doctor Wilson pulled the blanket down and examined him. He had a bullet wound in his chest near his heart.

"Looks like he died instantly," the doctor told them.

"Three more men are dead. What are you going to do about this, Sheriff?" Marvin Stringfellow asked, clearly upset.

"I'm the *sheriff*," Bullock said loudly. "I'll handle it!"

"Three *night-riders* with their hoods still on get hung. All three worked for Colonel Jessup," Jubal said angrily. "And now two *more* of his men kill one of my men and try to burn me out. It's as plain as the nose on your face he's the one behind all this!"

"I have heard and seen enough!" Marvin Stringfellow said loudly, his face flushed beet-red. "I want Colonel Jessup *arrested* and *charged,* Sheriff! If you won't do your job we'll get somebody that will! Is that clear?"

CHAPTER XI

Loud knocking on the front door woke Caroline from a deep sleep. *Who could be knocking this time of night?* She wondered. *Something terrible must have happened.*
In a few minutes she heard her father's voice from downstairs talking to another man. She couldn't make out the words, but from the angry tone of her father's voice it was clear something was wrong. Then her father and the other man went into the den and shut the door and she couldn't hear them any longer.
Alarmed at what must have happened, she slipped from her bed and quickly sleeved into her robe and stepped into her house slippers. She lit the bedside lamp and looked at the wall clock. It was four-thirty.

Had someone on the ranch been hurt? . . . or even worse? Maybe I could help, she thought.

Carrying the lamp, she quickly made her way downstairs to see what had happened. She approached the closed door of the den, which also served as her father's office. Before she could open the door she heard her father's loud, angry voice from inside.

"YOU BOTCHED ANOTHER RAID ON THE HAWK RANCH. . . AND NOW TWO MORE OF OUR MEN ARE DEAD? HOW COULD YOU LET THIS HAPPEN?"

Caroline stopped short with her hand only inches from the door knob. She stood with her hand covering her mouth in absolute shock at her father's words, not only by what he said but by the anger in his voice. She had never heard him so angry.

"It wasn't my fault, Colonel," the second man said. She recognized the voice as Vance Slade, their foreman. "Hawk's black slave sounded some kind of alarm. I shot him, but it was too late. The one called Jubal, his brother, and I don't know how many others poured from the house and started shooting. It was like they knew we were coming and were waiting for us. They cut down Blackie and one of the new men named Sam. The rest of us lit out!"

"WHAT KIND OF MEN HAVE I GOT WORKING FOR ME?" her father shouted. "YOU'RE SUPPOSED TO BE FIGHTING MEN, I PAY YOU FIGHTING WAGES! I EXPECT YOU TO DO WHAT I TELL YOU TO DO!"

"But Hawk's got *fighting men too.* You don't pay enough for a man to get hung."

Caroline couldn't believe what she was hearing! Her own father sending his men to murder the Hawk family and burn them out! She knew her father was a hard man—but *this?* She clamped her hand hard over mouth to stifle the sobs that threatened to erupt.

"That *Hawk* fellow's been nothing but trouble to me ever since he got back from the war," her father said angrily. "I'm going to get rid of him."

"How you planning on doing that?" Slade asked. "He's a tough hombre."

"I've sent for Trace Bonner."

"*Trace Bonner!*" the foreman exclaimed. "The *gunfighter*? He's nothing but a *paid killer!* I hear he's killed more'n twenty men.*"*

"He should be here any day now," Jessup said. "Then we'll be rid of Jubal Hawk once and for all."

Caroline had heard all she could stand; she turned and ran back up the stairs, closed the door, and flung herself across the bed, crying uncontrollably. Her mind was spinning, racing round and round, confused by what she had just overheard.

My father is plotting to kill Jubal! . . . Why? . . . Why would my father want to kill Jubal? . . . it didn't make any sense!

I can't allow that to happen! . . . I've got to warn Jubal!

Having made up her mind, she quickly dressed in her riding clothes, slipped down the stairs and out the back door. There was a light burning in the nearby bunkhouse and three saddled horses were tied to the hitching rail out front.

She quietly slipped past the bunkhouse and into the barn. She saddled her white mare and led her from the back door of the barn. It was still dark when she climbed into the saddle and walked her mount until she got out of earshot of the house.

Once a safe distance from the ranch, she heeled her mare into a gallop. She raced through the night. Her emotions were like a volcano building inside her; whirling, churning, threatening to erupt in a flood of tears.

Shock and anger tore at her. Her whole world had come crashing down with the sudden discovery that her father wasn't the man she had always thought he was. She had to stop this insanity! She had to warn Jubal about the killer her father had hired.

What was his name? Trace Bonner—yes—that was it—Trace Bonner the gunfighter.

* * *

Dawn was breaking. The entire Hawk family, along with Marvin Stringfellow, Doctor Wilson, and Sheriff Bullock, were gathered around the dining room table sipping coffee and discussing the recent events and how to deal with them.

Jason was standing beside the open front door with his rifle in the crook of an arm.

"Rider coming!" he suddenly called out, levering a shell. "It's somebody on a white horse. It looks like a woman."

At his brother's words Jubal jumped from his chair. He rushed to the front door and looked.

"It's Caroline Jessup!" he called over a shoulder to the others.

What in the world would bring her to the Hawk Ranch—especially this time of the morning? he wondered.

Everyone rose and followed Jubal and Jason to the front porch. Caroline reined up at the front gate. Jubal trotted to meet her and help her down—she was out of breath and sobbing uncontrollably!

"What's wrong, Caroline?" he asked quickly. "What's happened?"

"I've . . . I've . . . I've got something . . . something terrible to tell you," she choked out.

Jubal wrapped an arm around the sobbing girl's shoulder.

"Come in the house," he told her, guiding her toward the front door.

He helped her into the dining room and pulled out a chair.

"Sit down and tell us what's happened."

She slumped into the chair and buried her face in her hands.

The others gathered around and watched her with concern on their faces.

It took awhile for her to compose herself enough to relate what she had overheard. She held nothing back. When the telling was over she broke down again, sobbing uncontrollably.

Sarah Hawk put an arm around Caroline's shoulder and pulled her into her arms.

"You go ahead and cry, child," Mrs. Hawk comforted. "Get it out."

Jubal and the others were stunned at the story Caroline had related. They shook their heads in disbelief.

"I knew the Colonel was a hard man," the banker finally said, "but I would never have thought he would stoop to something like this. He's got to be stopped! He's got to be arrested!"

"I'll ride back into town and form a posse," Sheriff Bullock said. "I ain't about to try to arrest Colonel Jessup by myself."

"Do what you gotta do," the banker told him, "but see that he's locked up."

"What about the gunfighter he hired to kill Jubal?" Jason asked anxiously. "What are you gonna do about him?"

"I know the name. Every lawman in the country knows about Trace Bonner, but as far as I know, he ain't wanted for anything. Until he breaks the law there ain't nothing I can do."

Sheriff Bullock stalked from the house, mounted, and headed for town.

"I think it best that Caroline stays here until this is settled," Jubal told his mother quietly.

"Yes, I think you're right," Mrs. Hawk agreed. "There is no way she can return to that house until her father is locked up—it wouldn't be safe for her."

Jubal sat down beside Caroline and took her hand in his.

"Caroline, Mother and I think you should stay here until this is over."

Caroline thought it over for a long moment before reluctantly nodding agreement. "I don't see how I could go back there ever again," she said, again breaking down into tears.

* * *

They buried Washington Jefferson in the Hawk family cemetery later that afternoon.

The entire Hawk family stood around the fresh mound of dirt with heads lowered. Caroline stood between Jubal and Mrs. Hawk.

"He was as much a part of our family as if his name was Hawk," Sarah Hawk said.

The others all nodded agreement.

"He was a fine man and a faithful servant," Jubal said. "But more than that, he was a friend."

Jason had carved the name and date he passed on the cross-arm of a wooden cross at the head of the grave. Mrs. Hawk placed a bouquet of flowers on top of the grave.

As they were all returning to the house, Jubal took Caroline by the arm. "I need to ride into town. Will you be alright until I get back?"

Mrs. Hawk heard his words and paused to take Caroline's hand.

"She will be fine, won't you, my dear?"

Caroline lifted her eyes to Jubal and nodded.

"I'll be okay," she told him.

Jubal nodded.

"Watch out for things until I get back," Jubal told his brother. "I might be gone a day or two."

"I will," Jason assured him. "You ain't planning on going with the sheriff's posse are you?"

"No, I'm afraid it might just make things worse if I was there."

Sheriff Bullock still didn't have a posse put together when Jubal rode into Sweetwater. Only his deputy and one other fellow that Jubal didn't recognize sat their horses in front of the lawman's office.

He rode past the sheriff's office and continued to the livery. Jake Foley was shoeing a big bay work horse when Jubal reined up and climbed down.

"Hear the *night-riders* raided your place again last night," the blacksmith said, removing the horseshoe nails from his lips.

"Yep," Jubal acknowledged.

"I also hear it was Colonel Jessup's men that done it."

"Yep, we killed two of them. One fellow named Blackie Cain and nobody knew the other man. Jessup's daughter overheard her father and their foreman admitting they were the ones behind the raid. The sheriff's supposed to be trying to put together a posse to ride out and arrest Jessup and his foreman."

"Yeah, I know. He asked me to join up but I told him no. Most of the men in town are family men like me. They know trying to arrest Jessup and his foreman would most likely lead to gun play and don't want no part of it."

"Then what do you think the sheriff's gonna do?" Jubal asked.

"Don't know. Ain't no doubt Jessup's the one that got Bullock the sheriff's badge. Let's see what he does with it now that he's got it."

"Ever hear of a fellow named *Trace Bonner?*"

The blacksmith twisted a sudden, wrinkled eyebrow look at Jubal.

"Yeah, I've heard of him, he's a gunfighter, maybe the best there is. Why you asking?"

"Jessup's daughter overheard her father saying he had hired this Bonner fellow to kill me."

Jake stared at Jubal for a long minute before saying anything.

"Bonner is supposed to be bad—as bad as they come. He kills people for money. They say he's killed over twenty men. If I was you and I knew Bonner was coming after me, I'd make myself scarce—real scarce."

"In other words, *tuck my tail and run*? I can't do that. I've never run from anything in my life and I don't intend to start now."

"He'll kill you, Jubal."

"Maybe, but I'd rather die as a man than live as a coward. Anyway, there's something else I need to ask you. The *night-riders* killed Wash, our servant for over twenty years. I need someone to help around the ranch—a good worker—someone I can trust. Know anybody like that?"

Jake lowered his head and stroked his chin in thought. "Just might," he said. "There was a fellow passed through couple of weeks ago coming back from the war like you. His horse threw a shoe and he stopped to have it replaced. He asked if I might know where he could find work."

"Did you catch his name?"

"Yeah, I remember because his name matched him. Short . . . Carl Short. He seemed like a nice enough fellow."

"Did he say where he lived?"

"Matter of fact, he did. Said he had a few acres, a shotgun shack, a wife and two children waiting on him at home. He said his place was forty miles or so southeast on Coker Creek in the foothills of the Appalachian Mountains."

"Think I might ride down there and have a talk with him," Jubal said.

He thanked his friend and stepped into his saddle.

Jubal spent the night on the trail and found Carl Short's place at mid-morning the following day. Jake's description of the place had been right—it was a run-down, slat-board cabin that was in desperate need of repair. The small garden nearby was well-tended and a milk cow grazed on fresh, green grass. A team of plow horses also grazed nearby and a farm wagon sat inside the old barn.

"Hello the house," Jubal called, reining up a short distance from the house.

A man wearing faded and patched Confederate-issue pants and a work shirt stepped from a run-down barn with a rifle in his hands. Jubal judged him to be straddling forty or so. Jake's description of the man was accurate—he was a short man, standing barely over five foot. A grown boy beside him looked to be in his late teens.

"Can I help you mister?" the man asked.

"Looking for Carl Short."

"You found him. What can I do for you?"

"The blacksmith over in Sweetwater said you were asking about work."

"Yeah."

"Might be we could help one another. Know anything about horses?"

"Some. I know that's a mighty fine looking buckskin you're sitting astraddle."

"I'm Jubal Hawk. I've got a horse ranch not far outside Sweetwater. I could use some help."

"Light down and let's hear what you got to say," Short invited.

Jubal stepped to the ground and ground-hitched his buckskin.

"I understand you've got a wife and two children?"

"Yep. Charley here is seventeen. We've got a daughter named Claudette that's sixteen. My wife's name is Evalena."

"I see you fought for the Confederacy?"

"Yep. I served in the Army of Tennessee under General Braxton Bragg."

"I heard a lot about your outfit. You saw a lot of action," Jubal commented.

"More than I like to think about."

"Yeah, me too," Jubal agreed. "Carl, I need a couple of good men on the ranch. I'll pay top wages—thirty dollars a month apiece for you and your boy and furnish your family a cabin and keep."

Carl glanced quickly at his son and then back at Jubal. A wide grin broke across his face and he stuck out his work-hardened hand. "Mister Hawk, you just hired yourself a couple of hands. What we don't know about horses we're ready and willing to learn. When do we start?"

Jubal shook both of their hands to seal the bargain.

"You just did. I see you've got a team and wagon. Load your belongings and I'll be looking for you in a few days. Anybody in Sweetwater can tell you how to find my place."

Jubal mounted and glanced over his shoulder as he was riding away. Carl Short was patting his son on the shoulder as they hurried toward the house.

CHAPTER XII

Sheriff Sam Bullock was nervous. Despite his pleadings, he had only managed to convince three others, beside his deputy, to join his posse. He knew if Colonel Jessup refused to submit voluntarily to arrest and it came to a stand-off, he and his four men didn't stand a chance; they would be badly outnumbered and outgunned.

Marvin Stringfellow and Doctor Wilson had given the sheriff no choice—they were both members of the town council and had made it clear he either arrest Colonel Jessup or turn in his badge.

He liked being sheriff. He liked the power that came with the badge, but most of all, he liked the "extra money" he received each month from Colonel Jessup. He wasn't naive; he knew the money came with strings attached and that he was beholdened to the wealthy rancher, but so far, he had managed to keep the Colonel happy and keep his job to boot—but now he wasn't so sure—this latest incident put him in a tight spot.

Sully Hall, the new deputy he hired after he was forced to fire Deuce Bailey, rode up alongside the sheriff. Sam Bullock slanted a glance at the deputy. Sully sure wasn't the pick of the litter when it came to smarts, but he followed orders.

"How we gonna handle this, Sheriff?" the deputy questioned.

"Just keep your mouth shut and let me do all the talking."

"I mean, are we gonna ride in with our rifles ready or what?"

"NO, you idiot! You do that and you'll get us all killed! Keep your hands away from your guns! That goes for all of you!"

What I ought to do is turn around and forget this whole thing. I got a little money stashed away. I could start again someplace else. If we rub the Colonel the wrong way no telling what he's liable to do.

They were approaching the Jessup Ranch and from the sudden activity up ahead it looked like they had already been spotted. He saw Colonel Jessup and his foreman, Vance Slater, emerge from the house.

"Afternoon, Mr. Jessup, sir," Bullock greeted real friendly-like as they reined up in front of the big house.

"What are you doing here, Bullock?" Jessup demanded in a harsh voice. "I didn't send for you."

"Uh, well . . . we need to talk, Mr. Jessup."

"Talk? What have we got to talk about?"

"Well . . . sir . . . some things have happened that we need to talk about. Could we talk *privately*, just me and you?"

"Anything you got to say you can say right here, now what is it? You're wasting my time."

A huge knot lodged in the sheriff's throat. He swallowed, and then swallowed again, but the knot wouldn't budge.

This ain't going well, he thought. *This ain't going well at all.*

"Who are these *saddle tramps* you got with you?" Jessup demanded angrily. "Why are you bringing this *saloon trash* to my ranch?"

The sheriff managed to clear his throat and squeeze the words around the lump.

"Uh, . . . well . . . there was a raid early this morning out at the Hawk Ranch. Some men were killed and, uh . . . well . . . two of them were your men."

"Bullock, I have over twenty men working for me. I can't keep up with all of them *all* the time. What did they do, try to steal a horse or something?"

"No, sir, they . . . killed a man that worked for Hawk—a black man—and tried to burn Hawk's barn."

"A *black man?* All of this over a *black man?* What's one *black man* more or less? Why are you riding out here taking my time with this?"

"Well, you see, your . . . your daughter . . ."

"What's *my daughter* got to do with this?"

"Well . . . she . . . overheard you and your foreman talking . . . admitting you sent your men and . . . and that you hired the gunfighter, *Trace Bonner* to kill Jubal Hawk."

"Who *said* my daughter said that? Whoever told you my daughter said that is a *dirty, rotten liar!*"

"I heard her myself, Mr. Jessup. She was over at the Hawk Ranch and . . ."

"WHAT?" Jessup interrupted the sheriff with a scream. "MY DAUGHTER WAS AT THE HAWK RANCH? What was she doing there?"

"She was upset at what she overheard you and your foremen say. Marvin Stringfellow and Doctor Wilson heard it too. They forced me to come and . . . and arrest you and your foreman. I didn't want to, Mr. Jessup, but they made me do it."

Jessup swung a look at his foreman and broke out into loud laughter.

"You . . . you *think* you're going to *arrest* me?" Both Jessup and his foreman laughed out loud. A half-dozen other Box J riders standing nearby joined in their boss's laughter that the sheriff would actually think he could arrest *Colonel Jessup*.

The ranch owner suddenly cut his laughter off and fixed a hard stare at the sheriff.

"*How dare you* think you could just ride in here and *arrest me?* Now you listen to me, Bullock!" Jessup said through clenched teeth. "You take these *saloon drunks and get off my property* before I yank off that badge and cram it down your throat! YOU HEAR ME?"

Without a word Sheriff Bullock angrily jerked the reins of his horse around and rode away. The others in the posse followed.

Sam Bullock didn't say a word during the entire trip back to Sweetwater. When his deputy tried to say something to him, he received no reply. He reined up in front of the sheriff's office, dismounted and went inside. In less than five minutes he emerged with his belongings stuffed in his saddlebags, climbed on his horse, and rode out of town. Marvin Stringfellow found the sheriff's badge on the desk a few minutes later.

It was late afternoon just before sundown when Colonel John T. Jessup and a dozen well-armed riders thundered into the yard of the Hawk Ranch. Jason heard them coming. When he heard them rein to a stop at the picket fence that surrounded the house, he levered a shell into his Henry rifle and stepped through the front door.

Jason didn't have to wonder which of the riders Jessup was. The big rancher sat tall in his saddle on a golden palomino. His manner, long, gray hair, square jaw, and piercing eyes spoke of authority.

"I'm John T. Jessup. I want to talk to Jubal Hawk!"

"He's not here. I'm his brother, Jason Hawk."

"I understand my daughter is here. Send her out!"

"She's here, but she don't want to talk to you right now."

"It don't matter *what she* wants! I *said* SEND HER OUT AND DO IT RIGHT NOW!" Jessup shouted.

Jason quickly lifted his rifle to his shoulder and centered the sight on the center of Jessup's chest with his finger resting firmly on the trigger.

"You've worn out your welcome, Mr. Jessup. Now take your men and get off our property or I'll blow you outta your saddle," Jason said, his calm voice belying the raging storm going on in his stomach.

"I've got a dozen men here behind me, *boy!* They'll tear you and your whole family to pieces!"

"That might be, Colonel, but you won't be around to see it."

For a long moment that seemed like a lifetime, Jessup glared at Jason. Jason returned the look with his finger tightening on the trigger of his Henry. He felt perspiration on his forehead. The palm of his hand was suddenly wet with sweat.

"Alright," Colonel Jessup finally said. "You win this time, but we'll meet again, *boy*. Tell my daughter to get herself home."

Jason kept his rifle trained on Jessup as the big rancher reined his golden palomino around and signaled his men to follow.

Mrs. Hawk, Caroline, and sixteen year old Mary Lou Hawk walked from the house to stand beside Jason.

"Thank you for what you did, Jason," Caroline Jessup said. "I don't think I could face him right now."

"It was a brave thing you did, Jason," his mother told him. "Facing down a bunch like that."

A feeling of pride swept through Jason.

"Like Jubal always says, *a man's gotta do what a man's gotta do*."

* * *

After discovering that Sam Bullock had hastily quit as sheriff and high-tailed it out of town without a word, Marvin Stringfellow, as chairman, had called an emergency meeting of the town council.

"As you all know by now, Sam Bullock quit as sheriff. I'm sure we all agree that we're glad he's gone, but, because of the way it was set up by Isaac Lenoir when Sweetwater was founded, we, as the Sweetwater town council must appoint our own sheriff. He swept a look at the five members of the council gathered around a table in the bank: Jesse Hamburg, owner of the general store; Doctor Wilson, Sweetwater's doctor; Jake Foley, the blacksmith and livery owner, and Ray Muse, the barber.

"What are we gonna do?" Ray Muse asked. "We gotta have a sheriff."

"Anybody got any suggestions?" the banker asked, again sweeping a look around the table.

"We sure can't appoint Sully Hall to the job," Jesse Hamburg said. "He's a few bricks shy of a full load."

"We can't drag our feet on finding someone with all the bad stuff we got going on around here," Doctor Wilson said. "We've got to have a lawman that knows what he's doing."

"What about Ben Lambert?" Jake Foley suggested. "Don't know if he'd take it, but he served Sweetwater for several years before we replaced him with Sam Bullock. He's always been a good man and as far as I'm concerned, did a good job."

"Reckon he'd consider taking the job after the way we let him go before?" Doctor Wilson asked. "He's the only one around here that could stand up to Colonel Jessup."

No one at the table said a word for a long minute. They exchanged questioning glances.

"Wouldn't hurt to ask him," Jesse Hamburg said. "Far as I know he still lives out south of town. He was in my store a week or so ago."

"I'd be glad to ride out and talk with him about it if the council wants," Jake Foley told them.

"I make a motion we talk to Ben about the job," Ray Muse suggested.

"Do I hear a second to that motion?" Marvin Stringfellow asked.

"I second the motion," Doctor Wilson said.

"All in favor raise your hands," the banker said.

Everyone around the table lifted their hand.

"Alright then," the banker told them. "Jake, if you got time, ride out and talk with him and offer him the job."

"I will," the blacksmith said.

* * *

Ben Lambert was splitting wood when he saw Jake Foley riding up the road. He set the double-blade ax in a log and sleeved the sweat from his forehead as the blacksmith reined up.

"Howdy Ben," Jake greeted.

"Howdy, Jake. What brings you out this way?" Ben Lambert asked.

"Town council asked me to ride out and talk with you. The sheriff's job is open. We wanted to know if you'd consider taking it?"

"What happened to Bullock?"

"He just up and rode off without saying scat."

A belly laugh escaped Ben Lambert's mouth.

"Serves you right, I knew he was no good the minute I laid eyes on him."

"Ben, we made a mistake when we let Colonel Jessup talk us into letting you go and hiring Bullock. We feel real bad about it and we'd like you to come back."

"What's the job pay now-days?"

"Same as Bullock was making, sixty a month and all the fines you collect."

"That's better than I was making before."

"Something you ought to know before you decide," Jake told him.

"We've had some trouble here lately from a bunch of *night-riders*. They've been raiding some ranches in the county, running off stock and burning barns. They raided John Hawk's place. They burned him out and hung him."

"Yeah, I heard tell of that."

"Well, Jubal Hawk come back from the war and took over the ranch. He's rebuilt their house and barn and started over. They raided the Hawk place again and the next morning two of the *night-riders* were found hanging from a cottonwood just outside town."

"Ha, ha, ha," Ben laughed out loud.

"Turns out, both of them rode for Colonel Jessup. Him and his men was behind it all.

The council ordered Bullock to arrest the Colonel and his foreman and bring them in for trial. That's when he hightailed it out of town. He was obviously afraid to take on Jessup and his men."

Ben Lambert nodded his head and stared at the ground for a long minute.

"Never did cotton to Jessup. If I take the job will the town council back me up?"

"All the way," the blacksmith told him.

"Then I reckon you got yourself a sheriff."

They shook hands to seal the bargain."

* * *

Jubal reined up in front of the blacksmith shop late that afternoon.

"Did you find Carl Short?" Jake asked, as Jubal wrapped a leg around his saddle horn, doffed his hat, and mopped sweat from his hat band.

"Yep, he seemed like a nice fellow. I hired Carl and his seventeen year old son, Charley, too. Their whole family will be moving out to the ranch in a day or two."

"I've got some good news for you, too."

"Oh, what's that?"

"Sheriff Bullock up and rode off without saying a word to anybody. We think he didn't have the nerve to arrest Jessup and his foreman."

"That don't surprise me none."

"But I've got some more news that might. Ben Lambert is our new sheriff. I just got back from his place an hour ago. He'll start tomorrow."

"That *is* good news. Ben's a good man. He'll do a good job."

"We never should have listened to Jessup in the first place. He's the one that pressured the council to get rid of Lambert and hire Bullock."

"Well, what's done is done. I'm just glad Bullock is gone. I better be making tracks, I'm burning daylight. Adios, Jake."

"Watch your back, Jubal."

CHAPTER XIII

Caroline Jessup and Mary Lou Hawk spent a lot of time together. Although Caroline was two years older than Mary Lou, they had grown close in the two days since Caroline's arrival at the Hawk Ranch.

It was the *alone times* that were especially hard for her. Lying in her bed at night, the nagging questions returned: *Why had her father sent his men to hang Jubal's father and burn their house and barns and steal their horses? Why had he hired a paid killer to come and kill Jubal?*

Even growing up I knew he was a greedy man, but this? He always wanted the biggest and the best of everything, but I never thought he would actually have others killed to get what he wanted.

I can't go back there! I just can't! I don't know what I'm going to do, but I could never look at my father again without knowing what kind of man he is and what he is capable of.

Caroline and Mary Lou were in the barn grooming their horses when Jubal reined up just outside the barn and dismounted. Caroline saw him and felt her heart skip a beat. She forced herself to continue brushing her white mare as he walked his big buckskin up to the stall where she was.

"Are you okay?" he asked.

She twisted a look at him.

He is so handsome, she thought. *I've never met anyone like him.*

She nodded.

"I'm okay," she said softly. "I'm just very confused right now."

"I understand," he said. "Any way we can help, we'll be there for you."

"I appreciate what you've already done. I don't know what I would have done if you and your family hadn't helped. Mary Lou has been like the sister I never had."

"Well, you're welcome here as long as you want to stay."

"I don't know how I could ever begin to repay you."

Jubal smiled and led his buckskin toward an empty stall. Over his shoulder he said, "Your presence here is payment enough."

Caroline returned to her task of brushing her mare as Mary Lou joined her and leaned against the heavy boards of the stall. For a long minute the younger girl stared silently.

"He likes you, you know?" Mary Lou asked.

"What? . . . uh . . . What makes you think that?"

"It shows," the younger girl said, smiling broadly.

* * *

Jubal was unsaddling his buckskin when his younger brother walked up. He had his Henry rifle tucked comfortably in the crook of an elbow.

"Well, did you find someone to help on the ranch?" Jason asked, leaning against the stall.

"Matter of fact I did. Their name is Short. They seem like a nice family. They'll be here in a day or two. There's a boy about your age. His name is Charley. They have a daughter almost the same age as Mary Lou. They'll be moving into Wash's cabin."

"We had some visitors while you were gone. Colonel Jessup and a dozen of his men come calling."

Jubal's heart jumped and alarm spread through him.

"What happened? Is everybody okay?"

"Yeah, he said he come to get Caroline. I told him she didn't want to see him and wasn't going with him. He got hoppin' mad and said he was gonna take her anyway. I knew if it come to a fight I couldn't go up against the whole bunch.

"I was lucky enough to get the drop on him with my rifle. I didn't think he'd risk getting himself killed no matter how many men he had with him—I was right—he backed down—I sure was glad—I was scared."

"I'm proud of you, little brother; you did the right thing."

"Were you ever scared during the war?"

"Lots of times."

"Are you scared of the gunfighter Jessup hired to kill you?"

"Some, but I'll do what I gotta do."

"That means you're gonna face him, ain't you?"

"If it comes to that I'll face him. I wouldn't be much of a man if I ran."

"Can you beat him?"

"Probably not, I hear that's what he does for a living."

"Then I'll go with you. He couldn't beat both of us."

"No, if it comes down to that I'll do it alone."

Supper was over. The Hawk family lingered around the large dining table sipping coffee and discussing the new family that Jubal had hired.

"I look for them to be here in the next day of two," Jubal told the family.

"We'll need to get the cabin cleaned up and ready for them," Sarah Hawk reminded.

Caroline, watching Jubal from the corner of her eye, saw him drain his coffee cup and look in her direction.

"Would you like to go for a walk?" he asked.

Caroline swept a quick glance around the table, somewhat embarrassed. Her look settled upon Mary Lou for a brief instant. She saw an *I told you so* smile on her new friend's face.

"Yes," she said. "That would be nice."

Jubal rose and helped her with her chair.

Caroline stepped toward the front door, pulling a white shawl around her shoulders.

It was a beautiful evening. The air was crisp, yet comfortable. The black velvet sky twinkled with a million stars. A full moon smiled down at the couple as they strolled slowly toward the rail corral. Somewhere in the night a whip-o-will called to its mate. Off in the distance a mountain wolf howled its lonesome call.

They stopped at the corral fence. Jubal propped a booted foot on the bottom rail and stared up at the sky.

"Look," he said, pointing a finger at the moon. "See the cow jumping over the moon?"

"Where?" she asked.

He leaned closer and pointed again. She followed the direction he was pointing, but was very aware of his closeness. She could feel the warmth from his face only inches from hers. Her heart beat rapidly. Suddenly she felt his gaze fixed on her eyes. She turned her head to look into his eyes. Their eyes locked on one another—and held.

"I'm glad you're here," he said softly.

"Me too," she agreed.

Slowly, his hand lifted. His fingers brushed along her cheek as softly as the kiss of a butterfly. The thrill of that touch sent chill bumps racing up her spine. It was as if she had suddenly been transported to another world—another time—a time when nothing or no one else mattered except the two of them.

His face slowly lowered toward hers. Instinctively, she lifted her face to meet his. Their lips touched ever so gently, but the kiss sent a feeling surging through her she had never experienced before, racing to her heart.

My first kiss—Jubal is the first man that has ever kissed me.

It was unimaginably wonderful—far beyond even the fantasies she had fallen to sleep with ever since their first meeting.

Over the next several days the Hawk Ranch returned to something close to normal. Carl Short and his family arrived and settled into Wash's old cabin. Carl and his son, Charley, quickly adapted to the daily routine required to operate a horse ranch. Evalena and Claudette Short volunteered to assist Lilly and Myra Armstrong with the cooking and housekeeping chores.

Jubal and Caroline found occasions to spend time together, whether it was grooming horses, taking frequent walks after supper, or going on occasional rides to the waterfall.

It was apparent to all that their relationship was developing beyond that of mere friendship.

During one of their walks after supper, Jubal noticed that Caroline was unusually quiet.

"What's wrong?" he asked, as they walked hand in hand.

She didn't answer for a moment. When she finally lifted a look at him he saw small tears escaping her eyes.

"What's wrong, Caroline?" he repeated.

"It's just . . . I'm just worried, that's all."

"Worried? What about?"

"I'm worried about that gunfighter that my father hired to kill you."

"We'll cross that creek when we come to it. No use worrying about it."

"But . . . what if . . . I don't want to lose you."

"Worrying never changed nothing. I'll do what I gotta do."

"I'm so very sorry my father is like he is. He has changed into a man I don't even know any more."

"A lot of folks are still bitter about the war; I suspect that may be part of it."

"Please promise me you'll be careful?"

"I will," he said, nodding a promise.

* * *

The following day after their conversation, Jubal took the wagon, tied his buckskin behind it, and drove to town to get a load of feed from the store.

He backed the wagon to the loading dock of Jesse Hamburg's warehouse and told the store owner what he wanted.

"I'm gonna walk over to the sheriff's office and say *howdy* to our new sheriff," he told the store owner.

"We'll have your feed loaded when you get back," Jesse promised.

Ben Lambert was sipping on a cup of coffee when Jubal walked into the sheriff's office.

"Howdy, Jubal," the new sheriff greeted. "I heard you were back. Welcome home."

"Thanks, Ben. It's good to be back. I wondered more'n a few time if I was gonna make it back. It's good to see you with that badge back on."

"To tell you the truth, Jubal, it feels like I come back home too. Law work is all I've ever done. I feel like a fish outta water doing anything else."

"Reckon you heard about all the trouble with Colonel Jessup and the *night-riders*?"

"Yep, I heard. Fact is, I got a warrant right over there in my desk for Jessup and his foreman, Vance Slater. I've learned over the years to pick my time and place to fight my battles. I'll arrest them the next time they come to town."

"Ben, if you ever need my help, just let me know."

"I'm obliged, Jubal. I'm obliged, but if I get to where I can't do what I need to do, I'll hang up my gun."

As they talked, the door suddenly opened and a young man with a shiny new deputy badge pinned on his chest hurried in.

"Jubal, this is my new deputy, Gill Hodges. Gill, this is one of my old friends, Jubal Hawk."

Jubal and the new deputy shook hands.

"Sheriff, what I come to tell you was, that foreman from the Jessup Ranch is over at the saloon. He's got several of his men with him. Looks like four, best I can tell. You said you wanted to know if I seen him."

"You done right, Gill. Get that scattergun and come with me."

The sheriff withdrew the bone-handled Colt, checked the load, and replaced it in his holster.

"Mind if I tag along?" Jubal asked.

"If'n you're of a mind, you'd be welcome," Sheriff Lambert said, heading for the door.

The three of them walked side-by-side up the street toward the Ace-High Saloon. Ben paused at the bat-wing doors and looked inside before pushing them aside and stepping through with his Colt in his hand. The young deputy with the sawed-off scattergun followed his boss and stepped to one side once inside the large room. Jubal did likewise, stepping to the sheriff's right side and separating himself by several feet.

"Vance Slater!" the sheriff's deep voice rang out, filling the room. "You're under arrest! Stand up and raise your hands!"

The big foreman twisted a look over his shoulder, but remained seated. He held a drink in his right hand. His left hand rested on the table.

A brief moment passed. None of the foreman's four companions at the table moved a muscle.

"I won't be saying it again," Sheriff Lambert said, his voice as cold as tombstone.

The Jessup foreman slowly pushed to his feet and turned to face the sheriff, lazily lifting his hands shoulder-high.

"You're making a big mistake, Sheriff," the big foreman said.

"Use your left hand and toss your sidearm over here," the sheriff instructed.

The big foreman lowered his left hand and reached across his body and removed his pistol, tossing it across the floor in the sheriff's direction.

"Lefty, ride out to the ranch and tell the Colonel what's going on," the foreman told one of his men. "I'll be out before suppertime," the foreman bragged.

"Not likely," Sheriff Lambert said.

"The rest of you boys put your hands on the table palms down and don't move," Ben Lambert ordered. "Slade, you might give orders on the Box J, but not in Sweetwater. These boys ain't going nowhere except to jail."

The foreman's four companions did as they were ordered.

"Gill, collect their guns," the sheriff told his deputy.

Once the four Jessup riders were disarmed the sheriff motioned with his pistol.

"We're all gonna take a little walk down to the jail while my deputy takes a look-see in everybody's saddle bags. I'm sure hoping he don't find any toe-sack hoods."

Jubal helped Ben Lambert escort Vance Slade and his men to the jail. The sheriff herded them all into the small cell and locked the door.

"You done good, Ben," Jubal told the sheriff after they were back in the outer office.

"It felt like old times," his friend said. "I'm hoping Jessup will come in to check on his boys and give me a chance to lock him up, too."

"That's where he belongs." Jubal said.

"Jake told me about Jessup sending for the gunfighter."

"You ever heard about him?"

"Most everybody's heard of *Trace Bonner,* I reckon."

"Is he as good with a gun as they say?" Jubal asked.

"I ain't never seen him, mind you, but from what I hear, he's the best there is. If he comes, don't go up against him, Jubal, he'd kill you."

"I doubt he'll give me a choice. Well, I expect Jesse's got my feed loaded by now. I better be getting back to the ranch."

"Much obliged for your help," the sheriff said, sticking out a hand.

Jubal took his old friend's hand and shook it.

"You didn't need my help."

CHAPTER XIV

A day passed—and then two.

Of the five Box J riders Ben had arrested, his deputy found a toe-sack hood in all except the foreman's saddle bags. Nonetheless, he kept all five locked in the cramped cell with the hope their boss would come and try to get them out.

Ben Lambert stayed close to the office with his shotgun always within easy reach. The deputy patrolled the street, alert for any stranger or Box J rider.

It was mid-morning of the third day when they came. They charged into town at a hard gallop. Colonel Jessup led the way up the street on his high-stepping golden palomino. Seven riders rode behind him. Townspeople scattered out of the way and hid themselves in doorways and behind windows. The riders reined up in a line in front of the sheriff's office.

Ben Lambert stood in the doorway of his office with a double-barrel shotgun in his hands.

"You got some of my men, Lambert," the rancher said loudly. "I come to get them!"

"Afraid you're outta luck, Colonel. They're all under arrest. They're all part of the *night-rider* gang that's been tormenting folks hereabouts. We found their toe-sack hoods in their saddle bags."

"I don't care *what* you *claim* you found!" Jessup shouted, his face turning crimson-red. "Send my men out here!" he shouted, pulling his pistol and pointing at the sheriff. "I mean *right now!*"

"Climb down off that horse, Colonel!" Sheriff Lambert said, lifting his shotgun and thumbing back the hammer for both barrels. "I've got a warrant for your arrest, too."

"One word from me and my men will shoot you where you stand!" Jessup shouted defiantly.

"Maybe you best look around, Colonel," Sheriff Lambert said.

Colonel Jessup crooked a quick look over his shoulder and saw a young deputy off to one side with a scattergun pointed in his direction. His men were looking around nervously too.

"There's three more shotguns behind you," Sheriff Lambert told the rancher. "Now climb down off that horse before we get nervous and start emptying saddles."

All the *bravado* suddenly disappeared from the Colonel's demeanor, leaving a broken man, humiliated in front of his men and the townspeople looking on from doorways.

Slowly, he stepped down from his saddle and walked toward Sheriff Lambert.

Seeing their boss arrested, the rest of the Box J riders reined their horses around and rode slowly out of town.

"Make yourself at home, Colonel," the sheriff said, as he shoved the big rancher into the cramped cell with the rest of his men. "Judge Little will be in town in a day or two for the arraignment."

"I'll have your job for this, Lambert!" the big rancher shouted. "I've got the best lawyer in the state!"

"Looks like you might be needing him, Colonel," the sheriff said as he slammed the door and locked it.

"Send somebody to get the telegraph man," Jessup ordered. "I need to send a telegram."

The sheriff walked to the front door and looked up and down the street. He spotted Deputy Hodges a few doors away and motioned for him. Gill hurried to the sheriff.

"Would you mind going up to the telegraph office and ask Vernon to come down to the jail? Jessup wants to send a telegram."

"Be glad to," the deputy said, and hurried off.

Vernon Skinner showed up a few minutes later with a pad and pencil.

"Colonel Jessup wants to send a telegram," Sheriff Lambert told him.

A few minutes later the telegraph operator left with the message.

"We haven't got room to even sit down in here!" Jessup hollered from the jail cell.

"Then I reckon you'll have to stand up," Sheriff Lambert hollered back.

"You're going to pay for this, Lambert!" Jessup shouted. "Mark my words!"

"Stop your hollering if you boys want any supper," the sheriff told them.

That quieted them down for a while.

* * *

It had been three days since Sheriff Lambert arrested Colonel Jessup. The Colonel and his men were complaining loudly about the cramped quarters of the small jail cell.

Ben Lambert was pouring another cup of morning coffee when the door opened and a well dressed man entered. The sheriff sized the man up with a glance. He was short and heavy-set, with balding hair. He wore wire-rimmed spectacles that sat on the end of a bulbous nose.

"Are you the sheriff?" the man asked in a squeaky-sounding voice.

"I am. Name's Ben Lambert."

"I am Jacob Willhite, attorney at law from Nashville. I represent Colonel John T. Jessup. I would like to see my client."

The sheriff took down the keys from a wall peg and unlocked the door separating the office from the jail cell.

The attorney took one look and swung a critical look at the sheriff.

"Why do you have my client locked in that cramped cell with all those other men?"

"Cause that's the only cell we got in Sweetwater."

"That's *deplorable* and *inhumane!* I want my client released *immediately!*"

"Your *client* is charged with conspiracy to commit murder. He'll be released when the judge sets bail and not before."

"Who is the judge and where can I find him?" the attorney demanded.

"Judge Robert Little. His office is over in Madisonville. He'll be here tomorrow for the arraignment."

"Then I *demand* to speak with my client in private!"

"Mr. Willhite, you'll do a right smart better *asking*. We don't take kindly to *demands.*"

"Alright then, I'd like to speak with my client in private."

"Jessup," the sheriff hollered. "Step out here. Your attorney wants to talk with you."

Jessup stepped from the cell into the office. Sheriff Lambert locked the door behind him.

"I'll be right outside when you get your talking done," he told the attorney before stepping outside and closing the front door.

A half-hour later the door opened and the attorney stepped aside for the sheriff.

"We've finished for now. My client will need to *freshen up* before the arraignment."

"I'll see to it," Lambert said, unlocking the door to the cell and ushering Jessup back inside.

The following morning Sheriff Lambert escorted prisoner Jessup and his five men over to Jesse Hamburg's store and allowed them to purchase a fresh set of clothes. From the store, he took them to Marvin Sharp's Sweetwater Hotel where they took a bath and dressed in preparation for their court appearance.

Jubal sat beside Caroline Jessup on the first row behind the sheriff. Mary Lou Hawk sat beside Caroline with Jason beside his sister

Sheriff Lambert sat at the prosecution table. Colonel Jessup and his attorney were sitting at the defendant's table along with his men. Everyone rose when Judge Little entered. The judge scanned the courtroom with a glance and sat down.

"Be seated," the judge said.

The same county clerk Jubal had talked to in Madisonville rose and read from a paper.

"The county of Monroe, state of Tennessee versus John T. Jessup, Vance Slater, Benny Sand, Gus Worley, Otis Bull, and Blackie Cain. The Honorable Robert Little presiding."

"Mr. Jessup," Judge Little said. "You and each of your men are charged with conspiracy to commit murder. How do you plead?"

Jessup's attorney stood to his feet.

"Your Honor, my name is Jacob Willhite, attorney at law from Nashville. I am representing Mr. Jessup and his men. Each of them plead *not guilty* to all charges."

"Very well," Judge Little said. "Let me remind everyone that this is not a trial. This is simply an arraignment for the purpose of determining bail."

Sheriff Lambert rose to his feet.

"Your Honor, the defendant and all five of these men are charged with conspiracy to commit murder. We are concerned what additional crimes they might commit before their trial. We recommend all six of these defendants be denied bail and held until the trial."

"Your Honor!" Jessup's attorney jumped to his feet and raised his voice. "My clients have already spent four days in a tiny cell under *deplorable* conditions!

"John Jessup is an upstanding citizen and large property owner of this county who has never been charged with a crime of any sort. I recommend that he and his men be released under their own recognizance."

"It is the order of this court that all six defendants be released on their own recognizance until their trial," the judge said. "The trial will be held two weeks from today."

He pounded the table top with his gavel and stood. Everyone in the courtroom stood until the judge had left the room.

Jessup and his men shook their attorney's hand. Jessup turned and fixed a long stare at his daughter. Caroline lowered her head and refused to look at him. Jessup pushed toward her. Jubal stepped into his path and raised his hand.

"I want to see my daughter and talk to her!" Jessup said loudly.

"Your daughter don't want to see you or hear anything you have to say," Jubal said firmly.

"This is all *your* fault!" Jessup said loudly. "You stole my daughter from me!"

"No, she left to get away from *you!*" Jubal told him.

"Caroline!" Jessup hollered, as Jason and Mary Lou escorted Caroline away hurriedly. "CAROLINE! Don't do this to me!"

Jubal hurried to catch up with the others. Caroline was crying. It was the first time he had ever seen her cry—it broke his heart. He wrapped a protective arm around her shoulders and walked with her to their wagon.

CHAPTER XV

Trace Bonner lowered his head and pulled the collar of his black duster tighter around his neck against a chilly north wind. His high-stepping coal-black gelding pranced sideways up the narrow, dusty street of Sweetwater, Tennessee.

He paid little attention to the buildings on either side of the street—they would be similar to the buildings in any of the many towns he had been called to. He was here for one thing and one thing only—to do what he was paid to do.

He had long ago accepted his role as a paid killer and now it had become a source of pride—he was the best of the best and he knew it—savored it. There had been many who challenged his role, but they now lay in an unmarked grave in boot hill in some long forgotten town.

The name *Trace Bonner* spread fear wherever he went. Men stepped aside when he walked down the street. Women grabbed their children and hurried from sight. He had only to nod for men to quickly vacate their chair.

His arrival in Sweetwater didn't go unnoticed—it usually didn't—after all, his reputation reached far and wide. No lawman dared question his presence—no bounty hunter took up his trail.

His cold, pale-grey eyes flicked from side-to-side searching each alleyway, each rooftop, and every window. He knew he had many enemies—brothers, fathers, or other relatives of the many men he had killed. He knew that somewhere—sometime—a bullet would find him when he least expected it—but not here—not in a *nothing* place called *Sweetwater, Tennessee.*

He reined up at the hitching rail in front of the Sweetwater Hotel, glanced quickly up and down the mostly deserted street before slowly climbing from his saddle. He tied the reins to his gelding and untying his saddle bags, slung them across a shoulder. He slipped his Henry rifle from the saddle boot and climbed the steps to the porch of the hotel.

The soft jingle of his silver spurs and the thud of his boot heels on the wooden floor were the only sounds that disturbed the quiet of the hotel lobby as he approached the counter.

Marvin Sharp heard the sound and hurried in from a back room. He didn't have to wonder who the stranger was. One look told the hotel man who had just walked into his hotel. Trace Bonner's reputation had arrived long before the man. A sudden chill raced along the hotel owner's spine. He cleared his throat to remove the lump before words would come out.

"Can . . . can I help you, sir?"

"Need a room . . . upstairs . . . over-looking the street."

"Yes . . . Yes . . . Yes sir," Marvin Sharp stuttered, retrieving a key from the shelf behind him and laying it on the registration book on the counter.

"That will be room number four. Head of the stairs, turn right. Would you mind signing the register, sir?"

"See my horse gets to the livery, stalled and grain fed," the stranger said as he picked up the pen, scribbled a name in the book, turned, and climbed the stairs. Once he had disappeared from sight, Marvin Sharp turned the register book around and looked—sure enough there it was—the *infamous Trace Bonner* was actually staying right here in *his* hotel!

The hotel man hurried across the street to the sheriff's office and pushed open the door, out of breath.

Ben Lambert looked up as Marvin Sharp rushed into the office.

"It's him, Sheriff! It's *him!* He's right over yonder in *my* hotel!"

"Calm down, Marvin, you'll have a stroke. *Who's* over in your hotel?"

"*Trace Bonner,* that's *who*! He just now checked in."

Ben Lambert didn't reply. He merely nodded his head slowly.

"You go on about your business, Marvin, I'll handle it."

"Whatcha gonna do, Sheriff?" the hotel man questioned.

Ben Lambert removed his Colt from its holster, checked the load, and returned it to his holster on his right leg. He donned his Stetson and stepped from his office without bothering to answer the hotel man. Gill Hodges spotted the sheriff and hurried to catch up as he crossed the street.

"I saw him when he rode into town, Sheriff. It's that gunfighter, Trace Bonner ain't it?"

"Yep. It's him alright."

"You going to see him?"

"Yep."

"I'm coming with you," the young deputy said, opening his shotgun and checking the load.

Together Ben Lambert and his deputy entered the hotel. Marvin Sharp followed close behind them.

"He's in room number four, Sheriff."

The sheriff nodded and climbed the stairs with the deputy right behind him. When the sheriff reached the top of the stairs he motioned for his deputy to stay back.

"Wait here," he told his deputy quietly. "Don't do nothing unless you hear shooting, understand?"

Gill Hodges nodded understanding.

Ben Lambert approached room number four cautiously and rapped on the door.

"Who is it?" a voice from inside the room asked.

"It's Ben Lambert, sheriff of Monroe County. I need a word with you."

After a moment the door opened. The gunfighter held a pearl-handled Colt in his hand at waist level.

"What we got to talk about, Sheriff?" Bonner asked.

"Can I come in?" the sheriff asked.

Bonner opened the door wider and stepped aside to allow Lambert access. Bonner continued to hold his Colt on the sheriff. Lambert crossed the room to a ladder-back chair, spun it, and sat astraddle of it.

"You can put the gun away, Bonner. I just come to talk."

The gunfighter hesitated a moment before nodding his head and holstering his gun.

"I'm listening, Sheriff," Bonner said with his pale eyes fixed upon the sheriff.

"I know who you are and why you're here," Sheriff Lambert said. "I couldn't find a flier on you so as far as I know, you ain't a wanted man. So, *legally,* I can't run you out of town."

"How much they pay you to do what you do?"

"Not near enough," Lambert said, returning the gunfighter's long stare.

"I don't want to kill you, Sheriff, but I will if I have to. I'm here to do a job. I won't be leaving town until it's done. Are we clear on that?"

"Mighty sorry way to make a living if you ask me." the sheriff told him. "I know why you're here and I'm giving you fair warning. You break the law in Sweetwater and I'll either throw you in jail or kill you! Are we *clear on that*?"

"Sheriff, you got sand, I'll give you that," the gunfighter said, staring long at the lawman.

For a long minute Ben stared deep into the cold, pale eyes of a cold-blooded killer—one who would stop at nothing to do what he was paid to do. Without another word Ben Lambert pushed up from the chair, walked across the room, and out the door.

* * *

Three days after the arraignment, Ben Lambert rode out to the Hawk Ranch. Jubal was working in the barn and saw his lawman friend. He walked out to meet him.

"Mornin, Ben," Jubal greeted.

"Morning, Jubal."

"What brings you out this early in the morning?" Jubal asked.

"Got some news I figured you needed to know about," the lawman said.

"Oh?"

"Trace Bonner's in town, rode in yesterday."

"So Jessup really *did* send for him? I was hoping that was just a brag."

"Yep, he's here. I talked with him. No doubt about it, Jessup's hired him to kill you—he said as much."

"Ain't that grounds to arrest him or at least run him out of town?"

"Afraid not, he ain't broke any laws. Until he does there ain't a thing I can do. I rode out to tell you so you would stay out of town."

"Seems to me that wouldn't change anything. If he's bound and determined to face me down, he'll see it happens sooner or later."

"I suppose, but Jubal, as your friend I'm asking you not to face him. He's a cold-blooded killer—he'll kill you! I'm telling you—you can't beat him!"

"I'm much obliged for the information and your concern, but I'll do what I gotta do. I couldn't live with myself if I didn't."

"I was afraid that would be your answer," the sheriff said as he reined his horse around and touched thumb and finger to the brim of his hat.

I need to talk to Caroline and my family, Jubal thought, as he began to saddle his and Caroline's horses.

After both horses were saddled and waiting in front of the house, he went inside and found her.

"How about going for a ride with me?" he asked.

The question brought a wide, happy smile.

"I'd love to," she answered.

It was a beautiful day. The morning sun warmed them as they rode in silence for a ways.

"What's wrong, Jubal?" Caroline asked, reining to a stop. "I can tell something is wrong, what is it?"

Jubal stepped to the ground and helped Caroline from her horse before answering.

"Ben Lambert rode out this morning to tell me that Trace Bonner is in town."

"OH, NO!" she screamed, trying to stifle the cry with a gloved hand.

"I didn't want to tell you, but figured you had a right to know."

"Oh, Jubal, I'm so sorry, this is all my fault."

"No it isn't, Caroline. You had nothing to do with it. You were trying to help me by telling me about it."

"I'll go to my father and beg him to stop this! Maybe if I promise to come back, maybe he will listen to me!"

"It's too late, Caroline. It's gone too far to stop it."

"What are you going to do? You could leave; go far away where he couldn't find you."

"I couldn't do that. I'll have to face him. I have no other choice."

"I can't believe my father actually did this," she said angrily. "He actually hired someone to kill you!"

"Sure seems so. I've got to tell my mother."

"It will break her heart! You're going to face him, aren't you?"

Jubal answered her question with a single nod.

"When?"

"No use putting it off. I'll ride in this afternoon."

"Can I go with you?"

"I'd rather you didn't. I'll take Jason with me."

She suddenly threw her arms around his neck and buried her face in the hollow of his shoulder, crying. He held her until her weeping subsided. Lifting her head she looked deep into his eyes.

"Please don't go, Jubal," she begged. "I love you and I couldn't stand to lose you."

"I love you too, Caroline, but this is something I have to do. I couldn't live with myself if I didn't. Please try to understand."

She wiped the tears from her eyes and nodded acceptance of his decision.

Caroline went with him to tell his mother. He barely got the words out when she broke down, crying uncontrollably. She wrapped her arms around him; great sobs wracked her aging frame.

"NO! NO! I won't let you go! Please, Jubal! Please don't go! I lost your father; I couldn't bear to lose you too!"

He held her until the sobbing subsided. He kissed her on her tear-stained cheek.

"I'm sorry, Mother, this is something I've got to do."

He released her. Caroline and Mary Lou took his mother in their arms and held her close as Jubal hurried out the door. He wiped tears from his eyes as he set his ragged Confederate captain's hat on his head and climbed on his buckskin. Jason was already mounted with his shotgun resting in the crook of an arm. They rode side-by-side from the Hawk Ranch without looking back.

Jubal and Jason sat tall in their saddles as they walked their horses slowly down the dusty street of Sweetwater. They reined up at the Ace-High Saloon, stepped down, and tied their horses.

"This is my fight, Jason. I don't want you involved unless someone else joins into it, understand?"

Jason nodded understanding.

Jubal glanced over the top of the batwing doors and swept the room with a look. Only four or five cowboys sat around two tables, none of them looked threatening. Trace Bonner wasn't in the room. He pushed the batwings open and stepped inside. Jason stepped to the right and sat down at an empty table. Jubal walked to the long, polished mahogany bar that spanned the entire left side of the room. He removed his Confederate hat and laid it on the bar in front of him.

"Sam, get me a beer and then hurry over to the hotel and tell Mr. Bonner I'm here."

The heavyset bartender poured a mug of beer and set it in front of Jubal before hurrying from the room. Jubal slowly sipped the foamy liquid and watched the mirror behind the bar.

Five minutes passed slowly—and then ten before the batwing doors pushed aside and the gunfighter stepped into the room. Jubal took his measure from the reflection in the large mirror.

He was the picture of what Jubal thought a gunfighter would look like. He was tall and thin. His cheekbones pushed the pock-marked skin out until the bones were prominent, almost skeleton-like. His pale, flashing eyes were fixed upon Jubal's back as he moved cautiously to the far end of the bar.

For a long minute the gunfighter stared at Jubal. The room was stone-cold silent. No one moved—no one made the slightest sound.

"I didn't expect you to come," the gunfighter said in a voice barely above a hoarse whisper.

"I'm here," Jubal said firmly.

"You know why I'm here?" Bonner asked.

"I know," Jubal said.

"Nothing personal, it's what I do to make a living."

"Mighty hard way to make a living, I'd say," Jubal said.

Jubal's calm voice seemed to cause the gunfighter concern, but his voice belied the turmoil going on in his stomach.

It wasn't that he was afraid of dying—he had stared death in the face many times during his five years in the war. He knew his chance of outdrawing the gunfighter was near non-existent.

Suddenly a thought flashed into his mind—something his commander, Colonel John Mosby told him once.

"Captain Hawk, when you are faced with impossible odds on the battlefield, don't fight their battle—fight yours."

Trace Bonner frowned and looked hard into Jubal's unwavering eyes. He squared around facing Jubal. His right hand pushed back the long, black duster to reveal a pearl-handled Colt that rested in a tied-down black holster.

Jubal turned his body slightly. His left hand rested on the bar, his fingers touching the brim of his Confederate hat. His right hand dropped just below the holster on his right leg.

"I'm going to kill . . ."

The gunfighter never finished what he was about to say. A blast from underneath the Confederate hat punched a hole in the hat and sent it careening through the air. The .44 slug continued its deadly journey and punched a thumb-sized hole in the center of the gunfighter's chest. A second shot followed immediately and punched another hole only inches from the first.

Shock twisted the gunfighter's face into an ugly mask of death. His pale eyes went wide in disbelief. He staggered backward, his booted feet searching desperately for firm footing but finding none. His pearl-handled Colt fell from lifeless fingers and dropped to the floor.

First one leg and then the other doubled under him and he collapsed backwards to the floor.

The gunfighter's body had barely hit the floor when Sheriff Lambert rushed through the door with his pistol in his hand. His look flicked first to the dead gunfighter and then to Jubal. Jubal still held the smoking Colt in his left hand. His other Colt still rested in the holster on his right leg.

"Reckon he didn't know about you being ambidextrous," the sheriff said.

"Guess not," Jubal agreed, bending over and retrieving his Confederate hat and placing it on his head.

Jason walked up. Jubal put his arm around his brother's shoulders.

"Let's go home, little brother," Jubal said.

CHAPTER XVI

It was two days after the gunfight when Mary Lou and Caroline decided to go riding. Jubal watched as they saddled their mounts, happily talking and laughing. It made him feel good to see Caroline happy again.

"We won't be gone long, big brother," Mary Lou hollered over her shoulder as they rode away. Caroline twisted in her saddle to blow Jubal a kiss and wave.

Jubal busied himself with usual daily chores. He helped Jason, Carl, and Charley build another corral using lumber left over from their previous construction.

Noontime came and went, he figured the girls had decided to ride further than they intended, but as the sun drew closer to the western horizon he began to get concerned.

He hurriedly saddled his buckskin and climbed into the saddle. He heeled his mount in the direction he remembered the girls riding. Twilight came and went. A sick feeling churned in his stomach as darkness settled in.

He had ridden maybe two miles when up ahead he saw the profile of someone on foot—it was Caroline. He heeled his buckskin into a run.

Caroline tried to run to meet him but stumbled and fell. Jubal pulled the buckskin to a sliding stop near her and leaped from his saddle. He gathered the weeping girl into his arms.

"What happened?" he asked, deep concern filling his voice. "Where's Mary Lou?"

"They . . . they took her," she said through choking sobs. "The hooded men took her! I tried to fight them but they knocked me to the ground and took my horse."

"How long ago?" he asked desperately. "Which way did they go?"

"Toward the mountain, I think. It was about two or three hours before sundown. I've been walking so long I'm not sure."

Jubal knew it would be useless trying to track them in the dark.

"It's okay. Come on, I'll get you back to the ranch and get some help."

He helped Caroline into his saddle and climbed on behind. They galloped all the way back to the ranch. Fear . . . anger . . . guilt . . . all these emotions and more welled up inside him.

"Jason!" Jubal yelled at the top of his voice as they reined to a stop in front of the house.

Jason came running.

"What is it?" he asked anxiously. "What's the matter?"

"The *night-riders* kidnapped Mary Lou and set Caroline afoot."

"What are we gonna do, Jubal?"

"We're gonna find them, that's what we're gonna do! Ride into town. Bring the sheriff and as many of the others as you can. I'm gonna tell Mother and the others and then I'm gonna go looking. It'll be dark, but I'll find you when you get back!"

Jason hurriedly saddled his horse and galloped away. Jubal and Caroline hurried to the house to break the news to his mother. She broke down, crying uncontrollably.

"We'll find her, Mother," Jubal promised, secretly wishing he felt as confident as he tried to sound.

Carl and Charley quickly grabbed their rifles and saddled their horses. The three of them galloped out of the yard, heading toward the mountains. There happened to be a half-moon which offered sparse light, but not enough to follow a trail. Jubal knew it was useless trying to follow a blind trail in the dark—as bad as he hated to, he knew they would have to wait until morning.

"It's no use," he told his two companions sadly. "We'll have to wait until morning."

They walked their horses slowly back to the barn.

Jubal was quiet, lost in deep thought.

It's obvious Jessup is behind this. He must be a madman to try something like this. Where would he take her? Certainly not to his ranch, but where? Maybe the cabin where we found our horses—that's a possibility..

His mind searched for another answer, but none came.

"You boys stay here and wait for the sheriff. I've got this idea—probably just a wild goose chase, but I'm going to check it out. Tell Sheriff Lambert and his men to bed down in the bunk house and we'll try to pick up the trail come first light. I'll be back before then."

Jubal spurred his buckskin and headed off into the night at a gallop. In the dark it was hard finding his way back to the remote cabin where he and Jason had found their horses earlier. It took awhile, but he finally found it. A vague outline of the cabin was framed against the sky—it was pitch dark—not a sign of light. Nonetheless he rode forward. When he drew close he saw no horses in the makeshift corral—there was no one there. But to be absolutely sure he dismounted and pushed the remains of the door open—the cabin was empty.

It was a long and difficult ride back to the ranch. The eastern sky showed the faintest tinge of light as he wearily dismounted. There was a light in the bunkhouse as well as the "Big House." He could smell coffee brewing as he drew near the bunkhouse. Not surprisingly, a somber atmosphere permeated the room as Jubal stepped inside.

"Mornin'," Sheriff Lambert said, as he stomped on his boots.

Jesse Hamburg, Jake Foley, Ray Muse, Gill Hodges, Carl Short, Charley Short, and Jason were all there.

"Much obliged for coming," Jubal said, as he scanned the gathering of his friends. "I've been racking my brain where they might have taken her," Jubal told them. "Last night I checked a little cabin where I thought they might be, but found nothing."

An Indian stood in the background behind the others—Jubal had never seen him before. He wore homespun cotton pants, a loose-fitting blouse with a wide leather belt. He wore moccasins and his long hair was held in place by a beaded headband. A leather sheath attached to his belt held a bone-handled knife.

"Jubal," Ben Lambert spoke up. "I brought along a fellow I believe might help us. I've used him several times over the years. He's a Cherokee from over in North Carolina. In my opinion, he's the best *tracker* in these parts. If there's a trail—he'll find it. His name is Van Waite."

Jubal made his way over to the man and extended his hand. The man took it and pumped his arm once. Jubal felt his strong grip as they shook hands.

"I'm much obliged for your help," Jubal told him.

The Indian looked deep into Jubal's eyes and nodded.

"Let's saddle up," Jubal said.

As the light of dawn silently crept over the land, the armed riders headed out. The Cherokee rode in front, his dark eyes searching the ground with a wide sweep from side to side.

After they lost sight of the barn and corrals, the Indian raised his hand for the group to pause. He heeled his paint horse and rode off alone. Jubal and the others sat their saddles and watched—and waited.

Van Waite rode a wide circle of at least a quarter mile. They watched as he reined to a stop, slid nimbly from his horse, and knelt. They saw his fingers trace hoof prints before he stood and motioned the others to join him.

When Jubal and the others rode up, the Indian spoke for the first time.

"Two horses . . . go that way," he said, lifting an arm to point southward.

The tracker swung onto his horse and led the way, still keeping his gaze to the ground. They followed the trail for several miles.

"They walk . . . no hurry," the tracker told them.

Suddenly, he reined up and slid from his pony. Again, he knelt and closely examined the ground.

"Others come . . . struggle with women . . . ride off that way," he said, pointing north toward the mountains. "Other woman go that way on foot," he said, lifting an arm to point back toward the ranch.

"How many?" Sheriff Lambert questioned.

The tracker held up a hand with the fingers separated.

"Five?" Lambert asked.

The Indian nodded.

Again they followed the trail that led into the Little Tennessee River, but no tracks came out on the other side.

"They ride in water to hide tracks," the Indian said, pointing where the tracks entered the water.

"Let's split up," Sheriff Lambert suggested. "A couple of you fellows ride both sides of the river downstream. The rest of us will do the same upstream. Fire a shot if you find where they came out."

The posse members did as the sheriff suggested and rode away. It was near an hour later before one of the posse members upstream fired a shot. The rest of the posse rode to join him. Sure enough, the tracks left the river on a rocky shelf and headed north toward the foothills of the Chilhowee Mountains. The low hills were heavily wooded and slowed progress. Jubal knew that beyond the Chilhowee Mountain ridge lay the Great Smokey Mountain Range that stretched for hundreds of miles.

He knew if the kidnappers were in these vast mountains they would be hard to find. Still, his confidence in the Cherokee tracker was growing by the minute.

The sun was now directly overhead and their progress was painstakingly slow. Each time they came upon a mountain stream the tracks would completely disappear.

They sometimes had to search for an hour or more to find where the riders emerged from the stream—they were obviously trying to hide their trail from anyone who might follow.

By mid-afternoon they had climbed deeper and deeper into the mountains. The peaks reached far into the sky, seemingly touching the clouds. Their horses struggled to climb the steep grade. They were forced to pause often to allow their horses to rest.

At times the tracks were apparent. At other times the tracker had to search long and hard to pick up the trail. Sundown came and went. Darkness crept over the mountains and bathed the area in total darkness—they were forced to stop for the night.

The posse was up and on the trail by first light. By sunup they reached the summit of a high mountain peak. Suddenly the tracker pointed to the north. A pencil-thin trail of smoke rose upward, bent southward by a soft northern breeze. It appeared to be just beyond the next hogback mountain—no more than a few miles away.

"That's got to be them," Sheriff Lambert exclaimed, excitement obvious in his voice.

"Let's go," Jubal said, toeing a stirrup. "We ought to be able to get there before noon."

They descended steep mountainsides, their horses' hooves often sliding until they found footing. A stream laced through the wooded valley between the two mountains.

On the shoulder of the next mountain they glimpsed a log cabin—no more than a mile away. They watered their horses and tied them to low-hanging limbs. Taking their rifles, they climbed cautiously toward the cabin.

The smell of wood smoke reached them as they crept closer, careful to keep cover between them and the cabin. A split-rail corral contained seven horses. Jubal quickly recognized Mary Lou's brown and white pinto and Caroline's snow white mare. He also recognized the black and white pinto that belonged to the foreman, Vance Slade.

Sheriff Lambert motioned for everyone to gather around.

"Spread out and surround the cabin," he told them quietly. "Be sure to find cover in case it comes to a shootout. But remember, there's a girl in that cabin so, don't shoot unless you have to."

The men nodded and spread out, completely surrounding the cabin. Jubal and Jason took up positions behind a large outcropping no more that forty yards from the front door of the cabin. A small mountain stream no more than a few yards from the cabin furnished fresh water—it was perfectly located for a hunting lodge. The sweet smell of coffee and frying meat wafted through the mountain air.

When everyone was in place, Sheriff Lambert called out.

"Hello, the cabin! This is Sheriff Lambert from Sweetwater. You're completely surrounded! Throw out your weapons and come out with your hands empty and held high!"

From inside the cabin the sound of scurrying feet and shells being levered into rifles reached the hearing of the posse members. Then everything went quiet.

"Don't shoot!" a man's deep voice called out. "There's a woman in here."

"Send the woman out!" Sheriff Lambert called.

"Help!" a woman's voice that sounded like Mary Lou's called out.

"Shut your mouth!" a man's deep voice ordered, followed by the sound of an open hand on flesh.

"If you hurt that girl you'll curse the day you were born!" Jubal hollered.

"Jubal Hawk!" a deep voice called. "Is that you out there?"

"It's me, what you want, Slade?"

"We want you to drop all the charges and we'll let your baby sister go!"

"Let her walk out the door and we'll talk about it."

"We've got you surrounded, Slade!" Sheriff Lambert called out. "There's no way out! You've got a choice. Give up or die!"

The front door suddenly burst open. Three men with rifles firing blindly rushed from the cabin. They were met with a hail of rifle fire. The three kidnappers crumpled to the ground within ten feet of the door.

That only leaves Slade and one other, Jubal thought.

"Cover me!" Jubal shouted to Jason and the sheriff as he rounded the rocky outcropping.

A rifle shot from the window of the cabin ricocheted off the rock beside him. He heard the whine of a slug close to his face and felt its hot breath on his cheek.

Jubal raced across the forty yards that separated him from the cabin; he zigzagged from side to side. Rifle fire from behind him burst through the remaining glass of the window. Slugs from a rifle in the cabin gouged holes near his feet. He finally reached the cabin and pressed against the safety of the front log wall. He was panting heavily from the run and took a moment to catch his breath.

Shooting from the window suddenly stopped. For a long moment silence settled over the mountain. Without considering the consequences and thinking only of his helpless sister inside the cabin, he leaned his Henry rifle against the wall of the cabin, pulled both of his Colts from their holsters, thumbed back the hammers, and stepped to the front of the door. He lifted a booted foot and kicked the door in.

He purposely waited for the shots he knew would come—and they did—three of them in rapid succession. That's when he dove through the opening where the door used to be. He threw himself into a tumbling roll, searching the dimness of the room with a glance.

Fire blossomed from the muzzle of a rifle near the front window and gouged a furrow in the hard packed dirt floor. Jubal swung his left hand and returned fire. He heard a guttural groan. The shooter dropped his rifle and grabbed his stomach to stem a fountain of blood spurting through his shirt.

Mary Lou's shrill scream twisted Jubal's head toward the back corner of the small room.

He saw his baby sister arched backward in front of the big ranch foreman. Slade had Mary Lou's neck in the crook of his arm with her head pulled back. He had the nose of a pistol against her left ear.

"I'll blow her head off!" Slade shouted. "So help me, I'll kill her!"

"Okay, okay," Jubal told him. "Take it easy. Don't hurt her." Jubal pleaded, laying the Colt in his left hand onto the floor. He still had his other pistol in his right hand with the hammer back.

Suddenly Slade swung the pistol away from Mary Lou's head toward Jubal. The sudden movement by the foreman slightly separated him from Mary Lou. Jubal knew instinctively it was now or never—he feathered the trigger.

The Colt bucked in his hand. He heard a second blast at the same instant something slammed into his side with the force of a mule's kick.
　He felt himself slammed sideways. A white-hot pain shot through his left side. Suddenly he couldn't breathe.
　He heard a distant scream—it sounded like Mary Lou, but it was so far away. He heard other voices—felt gentle hands touching him. It was suddenly getting dark. The pain in his side suddenly subsided as bright lights exploded behind his eyes A swirling fog settled over him and the pain didn't hurt any more.
　I've been wounded. Where am I? I thought the war was over? I reckon I won't make it back home after all. Will they tell my folks I was killed on the battlefield? What battle is this anyway? There's been so many I've lost track. Was it a Yankee's bullet that got me? I'm so sleepy. My eyes won't stay open.
　A soft hand on his cheek slammed the door shut on his thoughts.
　Mother? Is that you? How did you get here?
　Blackness swallowed him and the sweet peace of unconsciousness ended the pain.

CHAPTER XVII

Pain screamed at him! Wracking his whole body! One minute he felt the jolting of movement that brought unbearable pain like he had never imagined—the next minute he was floating on a soft cloud somewhere above his own body—*but how could that be?*

Am I dead?—no, his numbed mind reasoned—*death wouldn't hurt this bad.*

Hazy images came and went. Time was endless and brought only more pain. Voices spoke to him in meaningless sounds that had no meaning. Blurred, unrecognizable faces flashed before his eyes and then disappeared.

Someone called his name. He struggled to answer and mouthed words, but no sound passed his lips.

Blackness . . . the sweet peace of blackness once again settled over him.

"Jubal," a voice he vaguely recognized called his name.
A soft hand touched his forehead.
"Can you hear me?" the sweet voice asked.
He struggled mightily to open his eyes. His eyelids were so heavy. With all his strength he struggled. A hazy, blurry figure took shape.
Who is it? I know I should know her. He blinked and blinked again—Caroline?
He felt soft lips brush his cheek and felt a hot tear drop onto his cheek.
"Welcome back," she whispered.
"Where . . . where am I?" he mouthed the words, but only a hoarse whisper came out.
"You're home. The doctor said you will recover, but it will take time."
"How long . . . how long has it been?" the whispered words sounded distant, jumbled to his own hearing.
"It's been a week," Caroline told him.
"How'd I get here?"
"The others made a travois and brought you here. You need to rest now; I'll explain everything when you're feeling better."

The days passed slowly and became a week—and then two. Someone was at his bedside night and day. He learned Doctor Wilson had removed the bullet from his side and sewn it up, but his broken ribs were mending slowly. He lost a lot of blood during the long trip from the mountain cabin to the ranch, but his mother's soup and chicken broth were restoring his strength quickly.

The doctor insisted he remain in bed another week in fear movement could do additional damage. Jubal was not one to stay in bed, but reason and Caroline's insistence kept him flat of his back.

Caroline had never mentioned her father and Jubal thought it better if he didn't ask.   She was careful to keep their conversations on a positive note.

Finally, he could stand lying flat of his back no longer and begged Caroline to help him sit on the side of the bed. The experiment was short lived, however, as he quickly became dizzy. The room started spinning and he had to lie back down.

It took another three days before he was able to join his family at the dinner table—it was a joyous occasion.

Another week and he was accompanying Caroline on short walks. They talked endlessly, laughed together, and occasionally spoke of the future, but she carefully avoided mention of her father.

Jubal's new hired hands were working out good. Both Carl and his son Charley were quick to adapt to the daily routine of running a horse ranch. Jason had voluntarily taken on the training workload while Jubal was recuperating.

Lilly and Myra Armstrong did the cooking and most of the housework. Sarah, Mary Lou, and Caroline kept the "Big House," as everyone called it, clean and also filled in with the chores of grooming the horses and general duties around the ranch.

Jubal was impressed at how well Caroline fit into the family—almost like she was one of them.

Jubal was sitting on the front porch swing one morning sipping coffee and watching Charley Short exercising one of their prime foal mares. Down the long, winding lane he saw Ben Lambert on his familiar gray barb. Jubal had always been impressed with the way the sheriff sat tall and straight in the saddle. Jubal lifted an arm to wave at his friend.

"You're out might early this morning," Jubal greeted.

"Thought I'd ride out and see if you're still *playing sick*," the sheriff joked.

"I think I've about rode that horse as long as it can run. Climb down and sit a spell. I'll get you a cup of coffee."

He climbed down and walked to the front porch to lean against a post before speaking.

"Don't mind if I do," the sheriff said, folding into a cushioned chair near the porch swing.

"Myra!" Jubal called loudly.

"Yes, sir, Master Hawk?" the maid answered from inside the front door.

"Would you mind bringing Sheriff Lambert a cup of coffee?"

"It be comin' right up," the young black servant replied cheerfully.

"You're looking mighty chipper," the lawman said. "Looks like you're on the mend."

"I oughtta be, it seems like I've been flat of my back a month of Sundays."

"You was hit bad. We were all worried you wasn't gonna make it."

"Still don't know what all happened up there," Jubal told him.

"It all happened so fast the rest of us didn't have time to be much help. I was on my way in the front door when I heard your sister scream and the two shots close together. That was some shot you made with your sister that close—

you nailed Slade right in the middle of his forehead. He was dead before he hit the floor.

"I saw you were hit bad and tried to stop the bleeding, but I knew if we was gonna have any chance saving you we had to get you back to a doctor. Some of the boys put together a travois. We loaded you on and got back as fast as we could, but you lost a lot of blood.

Doctor Wilson said he still don't know how you lasted that long for us to get you back.

"At least we cleaned out the *night-rider* bunch—*goodbye and good riddance.*"

"What happened at Colonel Jessup's trial? How'd that come out?" Jubal asked.

Ben twisted a look over his coffee cup and frowned.

"Didn't his daughter tell you?"

Jubal shook his head.

"No, for some reason she has avoided talking about her father."

"Well, maybe I'm talking out of school, but Colonel Jessup's dead. Somebody found him hanging from that same cottonwood just outside town one morning not long after our big shootout in the mountains."

Jubal was shocked! He sat there listening with his eyes wide and his mouth open.

"Yep, *somebody* put one of them toe-sack hoods over his head and a noose around his neck. They had his hands tied behind his back sitting on that golden palomino of his. The thing was, they had removed the bridle and left the horse to do pretty much what it took a notion.

"No telling how long it stood there with Jessup's neck stretched out before it decided to move around—course when it did, that was the end of the Colonel. So, in a way, I reckon you could say the Colonel hanged *himself.* Now who would have thought of that?"

"Do you know who done it?" Jubal asked.

"Nope, don't have a clue. More'n likely we won't *ever* know for sure. Got my own opinion, but that's all it is, an *opinion.* One thing I know for sure, it weren't *you.*"

"That's for sure," Jubal agreed.

"Well, I reckon we've chewed the fat long enough for one sittin'," the sheriff said, pushing to his feet. "Guess I better be moseying along. Oh, almost forgot, we had a stranger ride in a few days ago looking for the fella that killed *Trace Bonner.* Looked like a young, gunfighter *wanna-be.*"

"What'd you tell him?"

"Well, I fibbed a little bit and told him it was *me* that killed Bonner."

The sheriff chuckled.

"Seems like he lost interest kinda sudden-like and rode on down the road."

"I'm obliged for that, Ben."

"Good to see you up and around, Jubal."

"Much obliged for coming out, Sheriff."

* * *

"I'd like to go for a ride," Jubal told Caroline. "Would you join me?"

"Are you sure you feel up to it?" she asked.

"I think so."

They took their time saddling their horses and headed out just after noon. They rode slowly, both of them unusually quiet. After a while they found themselves at the waterfall on the river.

Jubal dismounted and helped Caroline to the ground. They walked slowly to the big boulder where they usually sat.

"Ben Lambert rode out for a visit this morning. He . . . told me about your father."

Caroline didn't reply for a long minute. She lowered her head. He saw her lips quiver.

Finally, she lifted her head and looked him square in the eyes.

"I've been trying to figure out a way to tell you. I'm sorry, I should have told you sooner, but you needed to get well and I didn't know how you might take the news.

"You and your family have been so good to take me in like you did; especially after all the trouble my family has caused you. I feel ashamed and responsible.

"For the first time in my life I've learned what being a *family* is all about. I see the genuine *love* your family has for one another—that's something our family has never had. In some small way I have felt a part of that and I hate to give it up, but it's time for me to go back home."

Jubal reached an arm and gently drew her close.

"I don't want you to go. I want you to stay and be a *real* part of the *Hawk Family.* I love you, Caroline. I think I've loved you since the first time I met you.

"*Will you marry me?*"

That silly little *grin* broke across her face and grew into a smile wider than a *country mile.* She wrapped her arms around his neck and pulled his lips to hers. Through the kiss she whispered,

"*Yes, Yes, Yes, I thought you'd never ask!*

THE BEGINNING

WANT MORE? . . .

If you enjoyed this book and would like to read more Dusty Rhodes books simply fill out the order form below, cut out of book and drop it in the mail with your check. Dusty will ship them within three working days. (or) visit Dusty's website listed below at: www.dustyrhodesbooks.com

___	**Man Hunter**	@ $18.00 = $_____
___	**Shooter**	@ $13.00 = $_____
___	**Shiloh**	@ $12.00 = $_____
___	**Death Rides A Pale Horse**	@ $12.00 = $_____
___	**Vengeance Is Mine**	@ $12.00 = $_____
___	**Jedidiah Boone**	@ $12.00 = $_____
___	**Longhorn I (The Beginning)**	@ $15.00 = $_____
___	**Longhorn II (The Hondo Kid)**	@ $15.00 = $_____
___	**Longhorn III(The Prodigal Brother**	@ $15.00 = $_____
___	**Longhorn IV(The Family)**	@ $15.00 = $_____
___	**Shawgo**	@ $15.00 = $_____
___	**Shawgo II**	@ $15.00 = $_____
___	**Chero**	@ $14.00 = $_____
___	**The Town Tamer**	@ $14.00 = $_____
___	**Death Angel**	@ $12.00 = $_____
___	**Hawk**	@ $12.00 = $_____

Please add $3.00 per book shipping charge = $_____

Total = $_____

Ship to: _____
Address _____
City _____ State _____ ZIP _____
Your e-mail address _____

Mail Order to: Dusty Rhodes
P. O. Box 7
Greenwood, AR 72936-007
Can be ordered on-line at: www.dustyrhodesbooks.com

THANKS FOR READING MY BOOKS!